OVERLOOKED

by

Maurice Baring

Dales Large Print Books
Long Preston, North Yorkshire,
BD23 4ND, England.

British Library Cataloguing in Publication Data.

Baring, Maurice
    Overlooked.

A catalogue record of this book is
available from the British Library

ISBN   978-1-84262-568-2 pbk

First published in Great Britain in 1922

Published in Large Print 2007 by arrangement with
A P Watt Literary, Film and Television Agents

Dales Large Print is an imprint of Library Magna Books Ltd.

Printed and bound in Great Britain by
T.J. (International) Ltd., Cornwall, PL28 8RW

OVERLOOKED

To
MAT

PART ONE

THE PAPERS OF ANTHONY KAY

CHAPTER I

When my old friend and trusted adviser, Doctor Kennaway, told me that I must go to Haréville and stay there a month or, still better, two months, I asked him what I could possibly do there. The only possible pastime at a watering-place is to watch. A blind man is debarred from that pastime.

He said to me: 'Why don't you write a novel?'

I said that I had never written anything in my life. He then said that a famous editor, of *The Figaro*, I think, had once said that every man had one newspaper article in him. Novel could be substituted for newspaper article. I objected that, although I found writing on my typewriter a soothing occupation, I had always been given to understand by authors that correcting proofs was the only real fun in writing a book. I was debarred from that. We talked of other things and I thought no more about this till after I had been at Haréville a week.

When I arrived there, although the season had scarcely begun, I made acquaintances more rapidly than I had expected, and most of my time was taken up in idle conversation.

After I had been drinking the waters for a week, I made the acquaintance of James Rudd, the novelist. I had never met him before. I have, indeed, rarely met a novelist. When I have done so they have either been elderly ladies who specialized in the life of the Quartier-Latin, or country gentlemen who kept out all romance from their general conversation, which they confined to the crops and the misdeeds of the government.

James Rudd did not certainly belong to either of these categories. He was passionately interested in his own business. He did not seem in the least inclined to talk about anything else. He took for granted I had read all his works. I think he supposed that even the blind could hardly have failed to do that. Some of his works have been read to me. I did not like to put it in this way, lest he should think I was calling attention to the absence of his books in the series which have been transcribed in the Braille language. But he was evidently satisfied that I knew his work. I enjoyed the books of his which were read to me, but then, I enjoy any novel. I did not tell him that. I let him take for granted that I had taken for granted all there was to be taken for granted. I imagine him to wear a faded Venetian-red tie, a low collar, and loose blue clothes (I shall find out whether this is true later), to be a non-smoker – I am, in fact, sure of that – a practical teetotaler, not without a nice discrimination based on the imagination rather than on experience, of French vintage wines, and a fine appreciation of all the arts. He is certainly not young, and I think rather weary, but still passionately interested in the only thing which he thinks worthy of any interest. I found him an entertaining companion, easy and stimulating. He had been sent to Haréville by Kennaway, which gave us a link. Kennaway had told him to leave off writing novels for five weeks if he possibly could. He was finding it difficult. He told me he was longing to write, but could think of no subject.

I suggested to him that he should write a novel about the people at Haréville. I said I could introduce him to three ladies and that they could form the nucleus of the story. He was delighted with the idea, and that same evening I introduced him to Princess Kouragine, who is not, as her name sounds, a Russian, but a French lady, née Robert, who married a Prince Serge Kouragine. He died some years ago. She is a lady of so much sense, and so ripe in wisdom and experience, that I felt her acquaintance must do any novelist good. I also introduced him to Mrs Lennox, who is here with her niece, Miss Jean Brandon. Mrs Lennox, I knew, would enjoy meeting a celebrity; she sacrificed an evening's gambling for the sake of his society, and the next day, she asked him to luncheon. In the evening he told me that Miss Brandon would be a suitable heroine for his novel.

I asked him if he had begun it. He said he was planning it, but as it was a holiday novel, and as he had been forbidden to work, he was not going to make it a real book. He was going to write this novel for his own enjoyment, and not for the public. He would never publish it. He would be very grateful, all the same, if I allowed him to discuss it with me, as he could not write a story without discussing it with someone.

I said I would willingly discuss the story with him, and I have determined to keep a record of our conversations, and indeed of everything that affects this matter, in case he one day publishes the novel, or publishes what the novel may turn into; for I feel that it will not remain unpublished, even though it turns into something quite different. I shall thus have all the fun of seeing a novel planned without the trouble of writing one myself.

'Of course you have the advantage of knowing these people quite well,' he said. I told him that he was mistaken. I had never met any of them, except Princess Kouragine, before. And it was years since I had seen her.

'The first problem is,' he said, 'why is Miss Brandon not married? She must be getting on for thirty, if she is not thirty yet, and it is strange that a person with her looks–'

'I have often wondered what she looks like,' I said, 'and I have made my picture of her. Shall I tell it you, and you can tell me whether it is at all like the reality?'

He was most anxious to hear my description. I said that I imagined Miss Brandon to be as changeable in appearance as the sky. I explained to him that I had not always been blind, that my blindness had come comparatively late in life from a shooting accident, in which I lost one eye – the sight of the other I lost gradually afterwards. I had imagined her as the lady who walked in the garden in Shelley's *Sensitive Plant* (I could not remember all the quotation):

'A sea-flower unfolded beneath the ocean.'

Still, and rather mysterious, elusive and rare. He said I was right about the variability, but that he saw her differently. It was true she was pale, delicate, and extremely refined, but her eyes were the interesting thing about her. She was like a sapphire. She looked better in the daytime than in the evening. By candle-light she seemed to fade. She did not remind him of Shelley at all. She was not ethereal nor diaphanous. She was a sapphire, not a moonstone. She belonged to the world of romance, not to the world of lyric poetry. Something had been left out when she had been created. She was unfinished. What had been left out? Was it her soul? Was it her heart? Was she Undine? No. Was she Lilith? No. All the same she belonged to the fairy-tale world; to the Hans Andersen world, or to Perrault. The Princess without ... without what? She was the Sleeping Beauty in the wood, who had woken up and remembered nothing, and could never recover from the long trance. She would never be the same again. Never really awake in the world. And yet she had brought nothing back from Fairyland except her looks.

'She reminds me,' he said, 'of a line of Robert Lytton's: "All her looks are poetry and all her thoughts are prose." It is not that she is prosaic, but she is muffled. You see, during that long slumber which lasted a hundred years–' Rudd had now quite forgotten my presence and was talking or, rather, murmuring to himself. He was composing aloud. 'During that long exile which lasted a hundred years, and passed in a flash, she had no dreams.'

'You mean she has no heart,' I said.

'No, not that,' he answered, 'heart as much as you like. She is kind. She is affectionate. But no passion, no dreams. Above all, no dreams. That is what she is. The Princess without any dreams. Do you think that would do as a title? No, it is not quite right. *The Sleeping Beauty in the World?* No. Why did Rostand use the title, *La Princesse Lointaine?* That would have done. No, that is not quite right either. She is not far away. She is here. She looks far away and isn't. I must think about it. It will come.'

Then, quite abruptly, he asked me what I imagined the garden of the hotel looked like. I said that I had never been here before and that I had only heard descriptions of the place from my acquaintances and from my servant, but I imagined the end of the garden, where I had often walked, to be rather like a Russian landscape. I had never been to Russia, but I had read Russian books, and what I imagined to be a rather untidy piece of long grass, fringed with a few birch trees and some firs, the whole rather baked and dry, reminded me of the descriptions in Tourgenev's books.

Rudd said it was not like Russia. Russia

had so much more space. So much more atmosphere. This little garden might be a piece of Scotland, might be a piece of Denmark, but it was not Russian.

I asked him whether he had been to Russia. Not in the flesh, he said, but in the spirit he had lived there for years.

Perhaps he wanted to see how much the secondhand impressions of a blind man were worth.

He soon reverted to the original subject of our talk.

'Why is Miss Brandon not married?' he said.

I said I knew nothing about her, nothing about her life. I presumed her parents were dead. She was travelling with her aunt. They came here every year for her aunt's rheumatism. Mrs Lennox had a house in London. She was a widow, not very well off, I thought. I told him I knew nothing of London life. I have lived in Italy for the last twenty years. I very seldom went to London, only, in fact, to see Kennaway. I told him he must find out about Miss Brandon's early history himself.

'She is very silent,' he said.

'Mrs Lennox is very talkative,' I told him.

'What can I call it?' he asked, in an agony of impatience. 'She has every beauty, every grace, except that of expression.'

'The Dumb Belle?' The words escaped me and I immediately regretted them.

'No,' he said, quite seriously, 'she is not dumb, that is just the point. She talks, but she cannot express herself. Or rather, she has nothing to express. At least, I think she has nothing to express: or what she has got to express is not what we think it is. I imagine a story like Pygmalion and Galatea. Somebody waking her to life and then finding her quite different from what the stone image seemed to promise, from what it *did* promise. At any rate I have got my subject and I am extremely grateful. It is a wonderful subject.'

'Henry James,' I ventured.

'Ah, James,' said Rudd, 'yes, James, a wonderful intellect, but a critic, not a novelist. The French could do it. What would they have called it? *La Princesse désenchantée*, or *La Belle revenue du Bois?* You can't say that in English.'

'Nor in French either,' I thought to myself, but I said aloud, '*Out of the Wood* would suggest quite a different kind of book.'

'A very different kind of book,' said Rudd, quite gravely. 'The kind of book that sells by the million.'

Rudd then left me. He was enchanted with the idea of having something to write about. I felt that a good title for his novel would be *Eurydice Half-regained,* but I was diffident about suggesting a title to him, besides which I felt he would not like it. Miss Brandon, he would explain, was not like Eurydice, and if she was, she had forgotten her experiences beyond the Styx.

CHAPTER II

I am going to divide my record into
chapters just as if I were writing a novel.
The length of the chapters will be entirely
determined by my inclination at the
moment of writing. When I am tired the
chapter will end. I don't know if this is what
novelists do. It does not matter, as I am not
writing a novel. I know it is not what Rudd
does. He told me he planned out his novel
before writing a line, and decided beforehand on the length of each chapter, but that
he often made them longer in the first draft,
and then eliminated. If you want to be
terse, he said, you must not start by trying
to be terse, by leaving out. You must say
everything first. You can rub out afterwards.
He told me he worked in charcoal, as it
were, at first.

I shall not work in charcoal. I have no plan.

I asked Princess Kouragine what Rudd was like. She said he had something rather prim and dapper about him. I was quite wrong about his appearance. He wears a black tie. Princess Kouragine said, '*Il a l'air comme tout le monde, plutôt comme un médecin de campagne.*'

I asked her if she liked him. She said she did not know. She said he was agreeable, but she found no real pleasure in his society.

'You see,' she said, 'I like the society of my equals, I hate being with my superiors; that is why I hate being with royalties, authors and artists. Mr Rudd can talk of nothing except his art, and I like Tauchnitz novels that one can read without any trouble. I hate realistic novels, especially in English.'

I told her his novels were more often fantastic, with a certain amount of psychology in them.

'That is worse,' she said, 'I am old-fashioned. It is no use to try and convert me. I like Trollope and Ouida.'

I offered to lend her a novel by Rudd, but she refused.

'I would rather not have read it,' she said. 'It would make me uncomfortable when I talked to him. As it is, as the idiot who has read nothing newer than Ouida, I am quite comfortable.'

I said he was writing something now which I thought would interest her. I told her how Rudd was making Miss Brandon the pivot of a story.

'Ah!' she said. 'He told me he was writing something for his own pleasure. I will read that book.'

I said he did not intend to publish it.

'He will publish it,' she said. 'It will be very interesting. I wonder what he will make of Jean Brandon. I know her well. I have known her for five years. They come here every year. They stay a long time. It is economical. She is a good girl. I like her. *Elle me plait.*'

I asked whether she was pretty.

The Princess said she was changeable –

journalière. 'Elle a souvent mauvaise mine.' Not tall enough. A beautiful skin like ivory, but too pale. Eyes. Yes, she had eyes. Most remarkable eyes. You could not tell whether they were blue or grey. Graceful. Pretty hands. Badly dressed, but from poverty and economy more than from *mauvais goût.* A very *English* beauty. 'You will probably tell me she is Scotch or Irish. I don't care. I don't mean Keapsake or Gainsborough, nor Burne-Jones, but English all the same. But I can't describe her. She has charm and it escapes one. She has beauty, but it doesn't fit into any of the categories.

'One feels there is a lamp inside her which has gone out, for the time being, at any rate. She reminds me of some lines of Victor Hugo:

"Et les plus sombres d'entre nous
Ont eu leur aube éblouissante."

'I can imagine her having been quite dazzling when she was a young girl. I can imagine her still being dazzling now if someone were to light the lamp. It could be lit, I know. Once, two years ago, at the races here at Bavigny, I saw her excited. She wanted a friend to win a steeplechase and he won. She was transfigured. At that moment I thought I had seldom seen anyone more *éblouissante*. Her face shone as though it had been transparent.'

Of course the poor girl was unhappy, and why was she unhappy? The reason was a simple one, she was poor, and Mrs Lennox economized and used her as an economy.

'You see that the poor girl is obliged to make *de petites économies* in her clothes. She suffers from it I'm sure. Who wouldn't? This all comes from your silly system of marriage in England. You let two totally inexperienced beings with nothing to help them settle the question on which the whole of their lives is to depend. You let a girl marry her first love. It is too absurd. It never lasts. I do not say that marriages in our country do not often turn out very badly. No one knows that better than I do, Heaven knows; but I say that at least we give the poor children a chance. We at least do not build marriages on a foundation which we know to be unsound beforehand, or not there at all. We do not let two people marry when we know that the circumstances cannot help leading to disaster.'

I said I did not think there was much to choose between the two systems. In France the young people had the chance of making a satisfactory marriage; in our country the young people had the chance of marrying whom they chose, of making the right choice. It was sometimes successful. Besides, when there were real obstacles the marriages did not as a rule come off. Mrs Lennox had told me that Miss Brandon had been engaged when she was nineteen to a man in the Army. He was too poor. The engagement had been broken off. The man had left the Army and gone to the colonies, and there the matter had remained. I didn't think she would have been happier if she had been married off to a *parti*.

'She would not have been poor,' said Princess Kouragine. 'And she would have been more independent. She would have had a home.'

She said she did not attach an enormous importance to riches, but she did attach great importance to real poverty, especially to poverty in the class of people with whom Miss Brandon lived. She said the worst kind of poverty was to live with people richer than yourself. It was a continual strain, she knew it from experience. She had been through it herself soon after she was married, after the first time her husband had been ruined. And nobody who had not been through it knew what it meant, the constant daily fret.

'The little subterfuges. Having to think of every cab and every box of cigarettes. Not that I thought of those,' she said. 'But it was clothes which were the trouble. I can see that that poor Jean suffers in the same way. And then, what a life! To spend all one's time with that Mrs Lennox, who is as hard as a stone

31

and ruthlessly selfish. She does not want Jean to marry. Jean is too useful to her.'

I said I wondered why she had not married. Surely lots of men must have wanted to marry her.

Princess Kouragine said that Mrs Lennox was quite capable of preventing it. She rarely took her out in London. She brought her to Haréville when the London season began and they stayed here two months. It was cheaper. In the winter they went to Florence or Nice.

I said I wondered whether she was still faithful to the man she had been engaged to, and what he was like.

Princess Kouragine said she did not know him. She had never seen him, but she had heard he was charming, *très bien*, but he hadn't a penny. It appeared, however, that he had a relation, possibly an uncle, who was well off, and who would probably leave him money. But he was not an old man and might live for years.

I said that perhaps Miss Brandon was

waiting for him.

'Perhaps,' said Princess Kouragine, 'but she was only nineteen when they were engaged, and he has been away for the last five years. People change. She is no longer now what she was then, nor he, probably.'

She did not think this episode was a real obstacle; she was convinced Miss Brandon did not feel bound, but she thought she had not yet met anyone whom she felt she would like to marry. Nor was it likely for her to do so considering the milieu in which she lived, in which she was obliged to live.

Mrs Lennox liked the continental, international world. The world in which everyone spoke English and hardly anyone was English. It was not even the best side of the continental world she liked. She did not mean it was the shady side, not the world of adventurers and gamblers, but the world of international 'culture'. All the intellectual snobs were drawn instinctively to Mrs Lennox. People who discovered new musicians, new novelists, and new painters, who suddenly pronounced as a dogma that Beethoven couldn't compose and that the old masters did not know how to draw, and that there was a new music, a new science, and, above all, a new religion.

'She is always surrounded just by those one or two men and women *qui rendent l'Europe insupportable et qui la gobent,* they swallow everything in her, her views on art, her dyed hair, and her ridiculous hats. Is it likely that Miss Brandon, the daughter of an old general, brought up in the Highlands of Scotland, and passionately fond of outdoor life, would find a husband among people who were discussing all day long whether Wagner was not better as a writer than a musician? She never complains of it, poor child, but I know quite well that she is *écoeurée.* She has had five years of it. Her father died five years ago. Till he died she used to look after him and that was probably not an easy life, either, as I believe he was a very exacting old man. Her mother had died years before, and she had no brothers and no sisters. No relations who were friends, and few women friends. She is alone in a world she hates.'

I said I wondered that she had not left it. Girls often struck out a line for themselves now and found occupations.

Princess Kouragine said that Miss Brandon was not that sort of girl. She was shy and apathetic as far as that kind of thing was concerned, apathetic now about everything. She had just given in. What else could she do? Where could she live? She had not a penny.

'You see if a sensible marriage had been arranged for her, all this would not have happened. She would have now had a home and children.'

I said that perhaps she was being faithful to the young man.

Princess Kouragine said I could take it from her that she had never loved, *'elle n'a jamais aimé.'* She had never had *a grande passion.*

I asked the Princess whether she thought

her capable of such a thing. She seemed so quiet.

'You have never seen the lamp lit,' said the Princess, 'but I have; only for one moment, it is true, but I shall never forget it.'

She wondered what Rudd would make of the character. He hardly knew her. Did he seem to understand her?

I said I thought he spun people out of his own inner consciousness. A face gave him an idea and he made his own character, but he thought he was being very analytical, and that all he created was based on observation.

'He certainly observes nothing,' said the Princess.

She asked who would be the hero. I said we had not got as far as the hero when he had discussed it with me.

'And what will he call the novel?' she asked.

Ah, that was just the question. He had discussed that at length. He had not found a title that satisfied him. He had got so far as *The Princess without any Dreams.*

'*Dieu qu'il est bête,*' she said. '*Cette enfant ne fait que rêver.*'

She told me I must get Rudd to discuss it with me again.

'Perhaps he will talk to me about it, too. I will make him do so, in fact. It will not be difficult. Then we will compare notes. It will be most amusing. The Princess without any dreams, indeed! He might just as well call her the Princess without any eyes!'

CHAPTER III

This afternoon I was sitting on a bench in the most secluded part of the park when I heard someone approach, and Miss Brandon asked if she might sit down near me and talk a little. Mrs Lennox had gone for a motor drive with Mr Rudd.

'He is our new friend,' she explained. 'That is to say, more Aunt Netty's friend than mine.'

I asked her whether she liked him.

'Yes, but he doesn't take much notice of me. He asks me questions, but never waits for the answer. I feel he has made up his mind about me, that I am labelled and pigeon-holed. He loves Aunt Netty.'

I asked what they talked about.

'Books,' she said.

'His books, I suppose,' I said.

I wondered whether Mrs Lennox had read them. I could feel Miss Brandon guessing my inward question.

'Aunt Netty *is* very clever,' she said. 'She makes people enjoy themselves, especially those kind of people... Last night he dined at our table, and so did Mabel Summer. You don't know her? You must know her, you would like her. She is going away tomorrow, for a fortnight to the Lakes, but she is coming back then. We nearly laughed at one moment. It was awful. They were discussing Balzac, and Aunt Netty said that Balzac was a snob like all – and she was just going to say like all novelists, when she caught herself up and said: "like Thackeray". Mr Rudd said that Balzac and Thackeray had nothing in common, and Mabel, who had caught my eye, and I, were speechless. Just for a moment I was shaking, and Mr Rudd looked at us. It was awful, but Mabel recovered and said she didn't think we could realize now the kind of atmosphere that Thackeray lived in.'

I said I didn't suppose that Rudd had noticed anything. He didn't seem to me to notice that kind of thing.

She agreed, but said he had moments of lucidity which were unexpected and disconcerting. 'For one second,' she said, 'he suspected we were laughing at him. Aunt Netty manages him perfectly. He loves her. She knows exactly what to say to him. He knows she is not critical. I think he is rather suspicious. How funny clever men are!' she said, after a pause.

I said she really meant to say, 'How stupid clever men are!' I reminded her of the profound saying of one of Kipling's women, that the stupidest woman could manage a clever man, but it took a very clever woman to manage a fool.

She said she had always found the most disconcerting element in stupid people – or people who were thought to be stupid – was their sudden flashes of lucidity, when they saw things quite plainly. Clever men didn't have these flashes, but the curious thing was that Rudd did.

I said I thought this was because, apart from his literary talent, which was an accomplishment like conjuring or acting, quite separate from the rest of his personality, Rudd was not a clever man. All his cleverness went into his books. I said I thought there were two kinds of writers: those who were better than their books, and of whom the books were only the overflow, and those who put every drop of their being into the books and were left with a dry and uninteresting shell.

She said she thought she had only met that kind.

'Aunt Netty,' she said, 'loves all authors and it's odd considering–'

She stopped, but I ended her sentence: 'She has never read a book in her life.'

Miss Brandon laughed and said I was unfair.

'Reading tires her. I don't think anyone has time to read a book after they are eighteen. I haven't. But I feel I am a terrible wet blanket to all Aunt Netty's friends. I can't even pretend to be enthusiastic. You see I like the other sort of people so much better.'

I said I was afraid the other sort of people were poorly represented here just now.

'We have another friend,' she said, 'at least, I have.'

'Also a new friend?' I asked.

'I have known him in a way a long time,' she said. 'He is a Russian called Kranitski. We met him first two years ago at Florence. He was looking after his mother, who was ill and who lived at Florence. We used to meet him often, but I never got to know him. We never spoke to each other. We saw him, too, in the distance once on the Riviera.'

I asked what he was like.

'He is all lucid intervals,' she said, 'it is frightening. But he is very easy to get on with. Of course I don't know him at all really. I have only seen him twice. But one didn't have to plough through the usual commonplaces. He began at once as if we had known each other for years, and I felt myself doing the same thing.'

I asked what he was.

She didn't quite know.

I said I thought I knew the name. It reminded me of something, but I certainly did not know him. Miss Brandon said she would introduce me to him. I asked what he looked like.

'Oh, an untidy, comfortable face,' she said. 'He is always smiling. He is not at all international. He is like a dog. The kind of dog that understands you in a minute. The extraordinary thing is that after the first time we had a talk I felt as if I knew him intimately, as if I had met him on some other planet, as if we were going on, not as if we were beginning. I suddenly found myself telling him things I had never told anyone. Of course, this does happen to one sometimes with perfect strangers, at least it does to me. Don't you think it easy sometimes to pour out confidences to a perfect stranger? But I don't expect people give you the opportunity. They tell you things.'

44

I said this did happen sometimes, probably because people thought I didn't count, and that as I couldn't see their faces they needn't tell the truth.

'I would find it as difficult to tell you a lie,' she said, 'as to tell a lie on the telephone. You know how difficult that is. I should think people tell you the truth as they do in the Confessional. The priest shuts his eyes, doesn't he?'

I said I believed this was the case.

'This Russian is a Catholic,' she said. 'Isn't that rare for a Russian?'

I said he was, perhaps, a Pole. The name sounded Polish.

No, he had told her he was not a Pole. He was not a man who explained. Explanations evidently bored him. He was not a soldier, but he had been to the Manchurian War. He had lived in the Far East a great deal, and in Italy. Very little in Russia apparently. He had come to Haréville for a rest cure.

'I asked him,' she said, 'if he had been ill, and he said something had been cut out of his life. He had been pruned. The rest of him went on sprouting just the same.'

I said I supposed he spoke English.

Yes, he had had an English nurse and an English governess. He had once been to England as a child for a few weeks to the Isle of Wight. He knew no English people. He liked English books.

'Byron, and Jerome K Jerome?' I suggested.

'No,' she said, 'Miss Austen.'

I asked whether he had made Mrs Lennox's acquaintance. Yes, they had talked a little.

'Aunt Netty talked to him about Tolstoi. Tolstoi is one of Mr Rudd's stock topics.'

I said I supposed she had retailed Rudd's views on the Russian. Was he astonished?

'Not a bit. I could see he had heard it all before,' she said. 'He was angelic. He shook his ears now and then like an Airedale terrier. Aunt Netty doesn't want him. Mr Rudd is enough for her and she is enjoying herself. She always finds someone here. Last year it was a composer.'

'Does Princess Kouragine know him?' I asked.

No, she didn't. She had never met him, but she knew of him.

I asked what Mr Rudd thought about Princess Kouragine.

'Mr Rudd and Aunt Netty discuss her for hours. He has theories about her. He began by saying she had the Slav indifference. Then Aunt Netty said she was French. But Mr Rudd said it was catching. People who lived in Ireland became Irish, and people who lived in Russia became Russian. Then Aunt Netty said Princess Kouragine had lived in France and Italy. Mr Rudd said she had caught the microbe, and that she was a woman who lived only by half-hours. He meant she was only alive for half an hour at a time.'

At that moment someone walked up the path.

'Here is Monsieur Kranitski,' she said. She introduced us.

'I have been walking to the end of the park,' he said. 'It is curious, but that side of the park with the dry lawn tennis-court, those birch trees and some straggling fir trees on the hill and the long grass, reminds me of a Russian garden which I used to know very well.'

I said that when people had described that same spot to me I had imagined it like the descriptions of places in Tourgenev's books.

He said I was quite right.

I said it was a wonderful tribute to an author's powers that he could make the character of a landscape plain, not only to a person who had never been in his country, but even to a blind man.

Kranitski said that Tourgenev described gardens very well, and a particular kind of Russian landscape. 'What I call the orthodox kind. I hear James Rudd, the writer, is staying here. He has a gift for describing places: Italian villages, journeys in France, little canals at Venice, the Campagna.'

'You like his books?' I asked.

'Some of them; when they are fantastic, yes. When he is psychological I find them annoying, but one says I am wrong.'

'He is too complicated,' Miss Brandon said. 'He spoils things by seeing too much, by explaining too much.'

I asked Kranitski if he was a great novel reader. He said he liked novels if they were very good, like Miss Austen and Henry James, or else very, very bad ones. He could not read any novel because it was a novel. On the other hand he could read any detective story, good, bad or middling.

Miss Brandon asked him if he would like to know Rudd.

'Is he very frightful?' he asked.

I said I did not think he was at all alarming.

Yes, he said, he would like to make his acquaintance. He had never met an English author.

'You won't mind his explaining the Russian character to you?' I said.

Kranitski said he would not mind that,

and that as his mother was Italian, and as he had lived very little in Russia and spoke Russian badly, perhaps Mr Rudd would not count him as a Russian.

Miss Brandon said that would make the explanation more complicated still.

CHAPTER IV

Life begins very early in the morning here. The water drinkers and the bathers begin their day at half past six. My day does not begin till half past seven, as I don't drink many glasses of the water.

At seven o'clock the village bell rings for Mass.

It was some days after the conversations I recorded in my last chapter I woke one morning early at half past six and got up. I asked my servant, Henry, to lead me to the village church. I went in and sat down at the bottom of the aisle. Early Mass had not yet begun. The church seemed to me empty. But from a corner I heard the whispered mutter of a confession. Presently two people walked past me, the priest and the penitent, I surmised. Someone walked upstairs. A boy's footsteps then clattered past me. The church bell was rung. Someone walked downstairs and up the aisle; the priest again, I thought. Then Mass began. Towards the end someone again walked up the aisle. I remained sitting till the end.

At the door, outside the church, someone greeted me. It was Kranitski. He walked back with me to the hotel. He asked me whether I was a Catholic. I told him that Catholic churches attracted me, but that I was an agnostic. He seemed slightly astonished at this; astonished at the attraction in my case, I supposed. He said something which indicated surprise.

I told him I could not explain it. It was certainly not the exterior panoply and trappings of the church which attracted me, for of those I saw nothing. Nor was it the music, for although I was not a musician, my long blindness had made me acutely sensitive to sound, and the sounds in churches were often, I found, painful.

I asked him if he was a Catholic.

'I was born a Catholic,' he said, 'but for years I have not been *pratiquant*, until I came here. Not for seven years.'

'You have not been inside a church for seven years?' I said.

'Oh yes,' he said, 'inside a church very often.'

I said most people lost their faith as young men. Sometimes it came back.

'I was not like that,' he said, 'I never lost my faith, not for a day, not for an hour.'

I said I didn't understand.

'There were reasons – an obstacle,' he said. 'But now they are not there any more. Now I am once more inside.'

'Inside what?' I asked.

'The church. During those seven years I was outside.'

'But as you went to church when you liked,' I said, 'I do not see the difference.'

'I cannot explain it to you,' he said. 'You would not understand. At least, you would understand if you knew and I could explain, only it would be too long. But as it was it was like knowing you couldn't have a bath if you wanted one – like feeling always starved. You see I am naturally believing. If I had not been, it would have been no matter. I cannot help believing. Many times I should have liked not to believe. Many times I was envying people who feel you go out like a candle when you die. I am not mystique or anything like that; but something at the back of my mind is keeping on saying to me: "You know it *is* true," just as in some people there is something inside them which is keeping on saying: "You know it is *not* true." And yet I couldn't do otherwise. That is to say, I resolved not to do otherwise. Life is complicated. Things are so mixed up sometimes. One has to sacrifice what one most cares for. At least, I had to. I was caring for my religion more than I can describe, but I had to give it up. No, that is wrong, I didn't *have to*, but I gave it up. It was all very embarrassing. But now the obstacle is not there. I am free. It is a relief.'

'But if you never lost your faith and went

54

on going to church, and *could* go to church whenever you liked, I cannot see what you had to give up. I don't see what the obstacle prevented.'

'To explain you that I should have to tell too long a story,' he said. 'I will tell you some day if you have patience to listen. Not now.'

We had got back to the park. I went into the pavilion to drink the water. I asked Kranitski if he was going to have a glass.

'No,' he said, 'I do not need any waters or any cure. I am cured already, but I need a long rest to forget it all. You know sometimes after illness you regret the *maladie*, and I am still a little bit dizzy. After you have had a tooth out, in spite of the relief from pain you mind the hole.'

He went into the hotel.

Later in the morning I met Princess Kouragine.

She asked me how Rudd's novel was getting on. I said I had not seen him, and had had no talk with him about it. I told her I had made the acquaintance of Kranitski.

'I too,' she said. 'I like him. I never knew him before, but I know a little of his history. He has been in love a very long time with someone I knew – and still know, I won't say her name. I don't want to rake up old scandals, but she was Russian, and she lived, a long time ago, in Rome, and she was unhappy with her husband, whom I always liked, and thought extremely *comme il faut*, but they were not suited.'

'Why didn't she divorce him?' I asked.

'The children,' she said; 'three children, two boys and a girl, and she adored them, so did the father, and he would never have let them go, nor would she have left them for anyone in the world.'

'If she lived at Rome, I may have met her,' I said.

'It is quite possible,' said the Princess. 'My friend was a charming person, a little vague, very gentle, very graceful, very musical, very attractive.'

'Is the husband still alive?' I asked.

'Yes, he is alive. They do not live at Rome any more, but in the Caucasus, and at Paris in the winter. I saw them both in Paris this winter.'

I asked if the Kranitski episode was still going on.

'It is evidently over,' said Princess Kouragine.

'Why?' I asked.

'Because he is happy. *Il n'a plus des yeux qui regardent au delà.*'

'Was he very much in love with her?' I asked.

'Yes, very much. And she too. He will be a character for Mr Rudd,' she went on. 'I saw him talking to him yesterday, with Mrs Lennox and Jean. Jean likes him. She looks better these last two days.'

I said I had noticed she seemed more lively.

'Ah, but physically she looks different. That child wants admiration and love.'

'Love?' I said. 'Won't it be rather unfortunate if she looks for love in that quarter? He won't love again, will he? Or not so soon as this.'

'You are like the people who think one can only have measles once,' she said. 'One can have it over and over again, and the worse you have it once, the worse you may get it again. He is just in the most susceptible state of all.'

I said they both seemed to me in the same position. They were both of them bound by old ties.

'That is just what will make it easier.'

I asked whether there would be any other obstacles to a marriage between them, such as money. Princess Kouragine said that Kranitski ought to be quite well off.

'There was no obstacle of that kind,' she said. 'He is a Catholic, but I do not suppose that will make any difference.'

'Not to Miss Brandon,' I said, 'nor really to her aunt: Mrs Lennox might, I think, look upon it as a kind of obstacle; but a little more an obstacle than if he was a radical and a little less of one than if he was socialist.'

She said she did not think that Mrs Lennox would like her niece to marry anyone.

'But if they want to get married nothing will stop them. That girl has a character of iron.'

'And he?' I asked.

'He has got some character.'

'Would the other person mind – the lady at Rome?'

'She probably will mind, but she would not prevent it. *Elle est foncièrement bonne.* Besides which she knows that it is over, there is nothing more to be said or done. She is *philosophe* too. A sensible woman. She insisted on marrying her husband. She was in love with him directly she came out, and they were married at once. He would have been an excellent husband for almost anyone else except for her, and if she had only waited two years she would have known this herself. As it was, she married him, and found she had married someone else. The inevitable happened. She is far too sensible to complain now. She knows she has made a *gâchis* of her life, and that she only has herself to thank. As it is, she has her children and she is devoted to them. She will not want to make a *gâchis* of Kranitski's life as well as of her own, and she nearly did that too. If he marries and is happy she ought to be pleased, and she will be.'

'And what about the young man who was engaged to Miss Brandon?' I asked.

'I do not give that story a thought,' said the Princess. 'They were probably in the same situation towards each other as the Russian couple I told you of were before they were married, only Jean had the good fortune to do nothing in a hurry. She is probably now profoundly grateful. How can a girl of eighteen know life? How can she even know her own mind?'

'It depends on the young man,' I said. 'We know nothing about him.'

'Yes, we know nothing about him; but that probably shows there is nothing to know. If there were something to know we should know it by now. It was all so long ago. They are both different people now, and they probably know it.'

I said I would not like to speculate or even hazard a guess on such a matter. It might be as she said, but the contrary might just as well be true. I did not think Miss Brandon was a person who would change her mind in a hurry. I thought she was one of the rare people who did know her own mind. I could imagine her waiting for years if it was necessary.

As I was saying this, Princess Kouragine said to me:

'She is walking across the park now with Kranitski. They have sat down on a seat near the music kiosk. They are talking hard. The lamp is being lit – she looks ten years younger than she did last week, and she has got on a new hat.'

CHAPTER V

During the rest of that day I saw nobody. I gathered there were races somewhere, and Mrs Lennox had taken a large party. Just before dinner I got a message from Rudd asking whether he might dine at my table.

I do not dine in the big dining-room, as I find the noise and the bustle trying, but in a smaller room where some of the visitors have their *petit déjeuner.*

So we were alone and had the room to ourselves. I asked him if he had been working.

He said he had been making notes, plans and sketches, but he could not get on unless he could discuss his work with someone.

'The story is gradually taking shape,' he said. 'I haven't made up my mind what the setting is to be. But I have got the kernel.

63

My story is what I told you it would be. The Sleeping Beauty in the Wood, but when the Prince wakes her up she is no longer the same person as she was when she went to sleep. The enchantment has numbed her. She will have none of the Fairy Prince; she doesn't recognize him as a Fairy Prince, and she lets him go away. As soon as he is gone she regrets what she has done and begins to hope he will come back some day. Time passes and he does come back, but he has forgotten her and he does not recognize her. Someone else falls in love with her, and she thinks she loves him; but, at the first kiss he gives her, the forest closes round her and she falls asleep again.'

I asked him if it was going to be a fairy tale.

He said, No, a modern story with perhaps a mysterious lining to it.

He imagined this kind of story. A girl brought up in romantic surroundings. She meets a boy who falls in love with her. This, in a way, wakens her to life, but she will not marry him; and he goes away for years. Time passes. She leads a numbed existence. She travels, and somewhere abroad she meets the love of her youth again. He has forgotten her and loves someone else. Someone else wants to marry her. They are engaged to be married. But as soon as things get as far as this the man finds that in some inexplicable way she is different, and *he* breaks off the engagement, and she goes on living as she did before, apparently the same, but in reality dead.

'Then,' I said, 'she always loves the Fairy Prince of her youth.'

He said: 'She thinks she loves him when it is too late, but in reality she never loves anyone. She is only half-awake in life. She never gets over the enchantment which numbs her for life.'

I asked what would correspond to the enchantment in real life.

He said perhaps the romantic surroundings of her childhood.

I said I thought he had not meant her to

be a romantic character.

'No more she is,' he explained. 'The romance is all from outside. She looks romantic, but she isn't. She is like a person who has been bewitched. She always thinks she is going to behave like an ordinary person, but she can't. She has no dreams. She would like to marry, to have a home, to be comfortable and free, but something prevents it. When the young man proposes to her she feels she can never marry him. As soon as he is gone, she regrets having done this, and imagines that if he came back she would love him.'

'And when he does come back, does she love him?' I asked.

'She thinks she does, but that is only because he has forgotten her. If he hadn't forgotten her, and had asked her to marry him, she would have said "No" a second time. Then when the other person who is in love with her wants to marry her, she *thinks* she is in love with him; she thinks he is the Fairy Prince; but as soon as they are engaged, *he* feels that his love has gone. It has faded from the want of something in *her* which he discovers at the very first kiss; he breaks off the engagement, and she is grateful at being set free, and glad to go back to her forest.'

I asked if she is unhappy when it is over.

He said, 'Yes, she is unhappy, but she accepts it. She is not broken-hearted because she never loved him. She realizes that she can't love and will never love, and accepts the situation.'

I said that I saw no mysterious lining in the story as told that way.

He said there was none; but the lining would come in the manner the story was told. He would try and give the reader the impression that she had come into touch with the fairy world by accident and that the adventure had left a mark that nothing could alter.

She had no business to have adventures in Fairyland.

She had strayed into that world by

mistake. She was not native to it, although she looked as if she were.

I said I thought there ought to be some explanation of how and why she got into touch with the fairy world.

He said it was perhaps to be found in the surroundings of her childhood. She perhaps inherited some strange spiritual, magic legacy. But whatever it was it must come from the *outside*. Perhaps there was a haunted wood near her home, and she was forbidden to go into it. Perhaps the legend of the place said that anyone of her family who visited that wood before they were fifteen years old, went to sleep for a hundred years. Perhaps she visited the wood and fell asleep and had a dream. That dream was the hundred years' sleep, but she forgot the dream as soon as she was awake.

I asked him if he thought this story fitted on to Miss Brandon's character or to the circumstances of her life.

He said he knew little about the circumstances of her life. Mrs Lennox had told him that her niece had once nearly married someone, but that it had been an impossible marriage for many reasons, and that she did not think her niece regretted it. That several people had wanted to marry her abroad, but that she had never fallen in love.

'As to her character, I am confirmed,' he said, 'in what I thought about her the first time I saw her. All her looks are poetry and all her thoughts are prose. She is practical and prosaic and unimaginative and quite passionless. But I should not be in the least surprised if she married a fox-hunting squire with ten thousand a year. All that does not matter to me. I am not writing her story, but the story of her face. What might have been her story. And not the story of what her face looks like, but the story of what her face means. The story of her soul, which may be very different from the story of her life. It is the story of a numbed soul. A soul that has visited places which it had no business to visit and had had to pay the price in consequence.

'She reminds me of those lines of Heine:

"Sie waren längst gestorben und wussten
es selber kaum."

'That is, of course, only one way of writing
the story I have planned to you. I shall not
begin at the beginning at any rate. Perhaps I
shall never write the story at all. You see, I
do not intend to publish it in any case.
People would say I was making a portrait.
As if an artist ever made a portrait from one
definite real person. People give him ideas.
But on the other hand it is my holiday, and
I do not want to have all the labour of
planning a real story, and at the same time I
want an occupation. This will keep me busy.
I shall amuse myself by sketching the story
as I see it now.'

I asked who the hero would be.

'The man who wants to marry her and
whom she consents to marry will be a
foreigner,' he said.

'An Italian?' I asked.

'No,' he said, 'not an Italian. Not a south-erner. A northerner. Possibly a Norwegian. A Norwegian or a Dane. That would be just the kind of person to be attracted by this fairy-tale-looking, in reality, prosaic being.'

'And who would the original Fairy Prince be?' I asked.

'He would be an ordinary Englishman. Any of the young men I saw here would do for that. The originality of his character would be in this: that he would *look* and be considered the type of dog-like fidelity and unalterable constancy, and in reality he would forget all about her directly he met someone else he loved. He would have been quite faithful till then. Faithful for two or three years. Then he would have met someone else: a married woman. Someone out of his reach, and he would have been passionately devoted to her and have forgotten all about the Fairy Princess.

'The Norwegian would be attracted by her very apathy and seeming coldness and aloofness. He would imagine that this would all melt and vanish away at the first kiss. That she would come to life like Galatea. It would be the opposite of Galatea. The first kiss would turn her to stone once more.

'Then being a very nice honest fellow he would be miserable. He would not know what to do. He would be a sailor perhaps, and be called away. That would have to be thought about.'

Then we talked of other things. I asked Rudd if he had made Kranitski's acquaintance. He said, Yes, he had. He was quite a pleasant fellow, no brains and very commonplace and rather reactionary in his ideas; not politically, he meant, but intellectually.

He had not got further than Miss Austen and he was taken in by Chesterton. All that was very crude. But he was amiable and good-natured.

I said Princess Kouragine liked him.

'Ah,' he said, 'that is an interesting type. The French character infected by the Slav microbe.

'What a powerful thing the Slav microbe

is; more powerful even than the Irish microbe. Her French common sense and her Latin logic had been stricken by that curious Russian intellectual malaria. She will never get it out of her system.'

I asked him if he thought Kranitski had the same malaria.

'It is less noticeable in him,' Rudd said, 'because he is Russian; there is no contrast to observe, no conflict. He is simply a Slav of a rather conventional type. His Slavness would simply reveal itself in his habits; his incessant cigarette smoking; his good head for cards – he was an admirable card player – his facility for playing the piano, and perhaps singing folk-songs – I don't know if he does, but he well might; his good-natured laziness; his social facility; his quick superficiality. There is nothing interesting psychologically there.'

I said that I believed his mother was Italian.

Rudd said this was impossible. She might be Polish, but there was evidently no southern strain in him. Although I knew for a fact that Rudd was wrong, I could not contradict him; greatly as I wished to do so I could not bring the words across my lips.

I said he had made Mrs Lennox's acquaintance. He said he knew that he had met him in their rooms.

I asked whether he thought Miss Brandon liked him.

Rudd said that Miss Brandon was the same towards everyone. Profoundly indifferent, that is to say. He did not think, he was, in fact, quite certain that there was not a soul at Haréville who raised a ripple of interest on the perfectly level surface of her resigned discontent.

Then we went out into the park and listened to the music.

CHAPTER VI

The day after Rudd dined with me I was summoned by telegram to London. My favourite sister, who is married and whom I seldom see, was seriously ill. She wanted to see me. I started at once for London and found matters better than I expected, but still rather serious. I stayed with my sister nearly a month, by which time she was convalescent. Kennaway insisted on my going back to Haréville to finish my cure.

When I got back, I found all the members of the group to which I had become semi-attached still there, and I made a new acquaintance: Mrs Summer, who had just come back from the Lakes. I know little about her. I can only guess at her appearance. I know that she is married and that she cannot be very young and that is all. On the other hand, I feel now that I know a great deal about her.

We sat after dinner in the park. She is a friend of Miss Brandon's. We talked of her. Mrs Summer said:

'The air here has done her such a lot of good.'

She meant to say: 'She is looking much better than she did when she arrived,' but she did not want to talk about *looks* to me.

I said: 'She must get tired of coming here year after year.'

Mrs Summer said that Miss Brandon hated London almost as much.

I said: 'You have known her a long time?'

She said: 'All her life. Ever since she was tiny.'

I asked what her father was like.

'He was very selfish, violent tempered, and rather original. When he dined out he always took his champagne with him in a pail and in a four-wheeler. He lived in an old house in the south of Ireland. He was not really Irish. He had been a soldier. He played picquet with Jean every evening. He went up to London two months every year – not in the summer. He liked seeing the Christmas pantomime. He was devoted to Jean, but tyrannized over her. He never let her out of his sight.

'When he died he left nothing. The house in Ireland was sold, and the house in London, a house in Bedford Square. I think there were illegitimate children. In Ireland he entertained the neighbours, talked politics, and shouted at his guests, and quarrelled with everyone.'

I presumed he was not a Radical. I was right.

I said I supposed Miss Brandon could never escape.

She had been engaged to be married once, but money – the want of it – made the marriage impossible. Even if there had been money she doubted.

'Because of the father?' I said.

'Yes, she would never have left him. She couldn't have left him.'

'Did the father like the young man?'

'Yes, he liked him, but regarded him as quite impossible, quite out of the question as a husband.'

I said I supposed he would have thought anyone else equally out of the question.

'Of course,' she said. 'It was pure selfishness–'

I asked what had happened to the young man.

He was in the Army, but left it because it was too expensive. He went out to the Colonies – South Africa – as ADC. He was there now.

'Still unmarried?' I asked.

Mrs Summer said he would never marry anyone else. He had never looked at anyone else. He was supposed, at one time, to have liked an Italian lady, but that was all nonsense.

She felt I did not believe this.

'You don't believe me,' she said. 'But I promise you it's true. He is that kind of man – terribly faithful; faithful and constant. You see, Jean isn't an ordinary girl. If one once loved her it would be difficult to love anyone else. She was just the same when he knew her as she is now.'

'Except younger.'

'She is just as beautiful now, at least she could be–'

'If someone told her so.'

'Yes, if someone thought so. Telling wouldn't be necessary.'

'Perhaps someone will.'

Mrs Summer said it was extremely unlikely she would ever meet anyone abroad who would be the kind of man.

I said I thought life was a play in which every entrance and exit was arranged beforehand, and the momentous entrance and the *scène à faire* might quite as well happen at Haréville as anywhere else.

Mrs Summer made no comment. I thought to myself: 'She knows about Kranitski and doesn't want to discuss it.'

'The man who marries Jean would be very lucky,' she said. 'Jean is – well – there is no

79

one like her. She's more than *rare*. She's *introuvable*.'

I said that Rudd thought she would never marry anyone.

'Perhaps not,' she said, 'but if Mr Rudd is right about her he will be right for the wrong reasons. Sometimes the people who see everything wrong *are* right. It is very irritating.'

I asked her if she thought Rudd was always wrong.

'I don't know,' she said, 'but he would be wrong about Jean. Wrong about you. Wrong about me. Wrong about Princess Kouragine, and wrongest of all about Netty Lennox. Perhaps his instincts as an artist *are* right. I think people's books are sometimes written by *someone else*, a kind of planchette. All the authors I have met have been so utterly and completely wrong about everything that stared them in the face.'

I asked whether she liked his books.

Yes, she liked them, but she thought they were written by a familiar spirit. She couldn't fit him into his books.

'Then,' I said, 'supposing he wrote a book about Miss Brandon, however wrong he might be about her, the book might turn out to be true.'

She didn't agree. She thought if he wrote a book about an imaginary Miss Jones it might turn out to be right in some ways about Jean Brandon, and in some ways about a hundred other people; but if he set out to write a book about Jean it would be wrong.

'You mean,' I said, 'he is imaginative and not observant?'

'I mean,' she said, 'that he writes by instinct, as good actors act.'

She said there was a Frenchman at the hotel who had told her that he had seen a rehearsal of a complicated play, in which a great actress was acting. The author was there. He explained to the actress what he wanted done. She said: 'Yes, I see this, and this, and this.' Everything she said was terribly wide of the mark, the opposite of what he had meant. He saw she hadn't understood a word he had said. Then the actress got on to the stage and acted it exactly as if she understood everything.'

'I think,' she said, 'that Mr Rudd is like that.'

I asked Mrs Summer if she knew Kranitski.

'Just a little,' she said. 'What do you think about him?'

I said I liked him.

'He's very quick and easy to get on with,' she said.

'Like all Russians.'

'Like all Russians, but I don't think he's quite like all Russians, at least not the kind of Russians one meets.'

'No, more like the Russians one doesn't meet.'

'Tolstoi's Russians. Yes. It's a pity they have such a genius for unhappiness.'

I said I thought Kranitski did not seem unhappy.

'No, but more as if he had just recovered than if he was quite well.'

I said I thought he gave one the impression that he was capable of being very happy. There was nothing gloomy about him.

'All people who are unhappy are generally very happy, too,' she said, 'at least they are often very...'

'Gay?' I suggested.

She agreed.

I said I thought he was more than an unhappy person with high spirits, which one saw often enough. He gave me the impression of a person capable of *solid* happiness, the kind of business-like happiness that comes from a fundamental goodness.

'Yes, he might be like that,' she said, 'only one doesn't know quite what his life has been and is.'

She meant she knew all too well that his life had not been one in which happiness was possible.

I agreed.

'One knows so little about other people.'

'Nothing,' I said. 'Perhaps he is miserable.

He ought to marry. I feel he is very domestic.'

'I sometimes think,' she said, 'that the people who marry – the men I mean – are those who want the help and support of a woman, women are so far stronger and braver than men; and that those who don't marry are sometimes those who are strong enough to face life without this help. Of course, there are others who aren't either strong enough or weak enough to need it, but they don't matter.'

I said I supposed she thought Kranitski would be strong enough to do without marriage.

'I think so,' she said, 'but then, I hardly know him.'

'Does your theory apply to women, too?' I asked. 'Are there some women who are strong enough to face life alone?'

She said women were strong enough to do either. In either case life was for them just as difficult.

I asked if she thought Miss Brandon

would be happier married or not married.

'Jean would never marry unless she married the right person, the man she wanted to marry,' she said.

'Would the person she wanted to marry,' I said, 'necessarily be the right person?'

'He would be more right for her, whatever the drawbacks, than anyone else.'

I said I supposed nearly everyone thought they were marrying the right person, and yet how strangely most marriages turned out.

'Nothing better than marriage has been invented, all the same,' she said, 'and if people marry when they are old enough...'

'To know better,' I said.

'Yes, it doesn't then turn out so very badly as a rule.'

I said that as things were at present Miss Brandon's life seemed to me completely wasted.

'So it is, but it might be worse. It might be a tragedy. Supposing she married someone who became fond of someone else.'

'She would mind,' I said.

'She would mind terribly.'

I said I thought people always got what they wanted in the long run. If she wanted a marriage of a definite kind she would probably end by getting it.

Mrs Summer agreed in the main, but she thought that although one often did get what one wanted in the long run, it often came either too late or not quite at the moment when one wanted it, or one found when one had got it that it was after all not quite what one had wanted.

'Then,' I said, 'you think it is no use wanting anything?'

'No use,' she said, 'no use whatever.'

'You are a pessimist.'

'I am old enough to have no illusions.'

'But you want other people to have illusions?'

'I think there is such a thing as happiness in the world, and that when you see someone who might be happy, missing the chance of it, it's a pity. That's all.'

Then I said:

'You want other people to want things.'

'Other people? Yes,' she said. 'Quite dreadfully I want it.'

At that moment Mrs Lennox came up to us and said:

'I have won five hundred francs, and I had the courage to leave the Casino. I can't think what has happened to Jean. I have been looking for her the whole evening.'

I left them and went into the hotel.

CHAPTER VII

It was the morning after the conversation I had with Mrs Summer that I received a message from Miss Brandon. She wanted to speak to me. Could I be, about five o'clock, at the end of the alley? I was punctual at the rendezvous.

'I wanted to have a talk,' she said, 'today, if possible, because tomorrow Aunt Netty has organized an expedition to the lakes, and the day after we are all going to the races, so I didn't know when I should see you again.'

'But you are not going away yet, are you?' I asked.

No, they were not going away, they would very likely stay on till the end of July. Then there was an idea of Switzerland; or perhaps the Mozart festival at Munich, followed by a week at Bayreuth. Mr Rudd was going to Bayreuth, and had convinced Mrs Lennox that she was a Wagnerite.

'I thought you couldn't be going away yet – but one never knows, here people disappear so suddenly, and I wanted to see you so particularly and at once. You are going to finish your cure?'

I said my time limit was another fortnight. After that I was going back to my villa at Cadenabbia.

'Shall you come here next year?'

I said it depended on my doctor. I asked her her plans.

'I don't think I shall come back next year.'

There was a slight note of suppressed exultation in her voice. I asked whether Mrs Lennox was tired of Haréville.

'Aunt Netty loves it, better than ever. Mr Rudd has promised her to come too.'

There was a long pause.

'I can't bear it any longer,' she said at last.

'Haréville?'

'Haréville and all of it – everything.'

There was another long pause. She broke it.

'You talked to Mabel Summer yesterday?'

I said we had had a long talk.

'I'm sure you liked her?'

I said I had found her delightful.

'She's my oldest friend, although she's older than I am. Poor Mabel, she's had a very unhappy life.'

I said one felt in her the sympathy that came from experience.

'Oh yes, she's so brave; she's wonderful.'

I said I supposed she'd had great disappointments.

'More than that. Tragedies. One thing after another.'

I asked whether she had any children.

'Her two little girls both died when they were babies. But it wasn't that. She'll tell you all about it, perhaps, some day.'

I said I doubted whether we would ever meet again.

'Mabel always keeps up with everybody she makes friends with. She doesn't often make new friends. She told me she had made two new friends here. You and Kranitski.'

'She likes him?' I said.

'She likes him very much. She's very fastidious, very hard to please, very critical.'

I said everyone seemed to like Kranitski.

'Aunt Netty says he's commonplace, but that's because Mr Rudd said he was commonplace.'

I said Rudd always had theories about people.

'You like Mr Rudd?' she asked.

I said I did, and reminded her that she had told me she did.

'If you want to know the truth,' she said, 'I don't. I think he's awful.' She laughed. 'Isn't it funny? A week ago I would have rather died than admit this to you, but now I don't care. Of course I know he's a good writer and clever and subtle, and all that – but I've come to the conclusion–'

'To what conclusion?'

'Well, that I don't – that I like the other sort of people better.'

'The stupid people?'

'No.'

'The clever people?'

'No.'

'What people?'

'I don't know. Nice people.'

'People like–'

'People like Mabel Summer and Princess Kouragine,' she interrupted.

'They are both very clever, I think,' I said.

'Yes, but it's not that that matters.'

I said I thought intelligence mattered a great deal.

'When it's natural,' she said.

'Do you think people can become religious if they're not?' she asked suddenly.

I said that I didn't feel that I could, but it certainly did happen to some people.

'I'm afraid it will never happen to me,' she said. 'I used to hope it might never happen, but now I hope the opposite. Last night, after you went in, Aunt Netty took us to the café, and we all sat there: Mr Rudd, Mabel, a Frenchman whose name I don't know, and M. Kranitski. The Frenchman was talking about China, and said he had stayed with a French priest there. The priest had asked him why he didn't go to Mass. The Frenchman said he had no faith. The priest had said it was quite simple, he had only to pray to the Sante Vierge for faith. *'Mon enfant, c'est bien simple: il faut demander la foi à la Sainte Vierge.'* He said this, imitating the priest, in a falsetto voice. They all laughed except M. Kranitski, who said, seriously, 'Of course, you should ask the Sante Vierge.' When the Frenchman and M. Kranitski went away, Mr Rudd said that in matters of religion Russians were childish, and that M. Kranitski has a *simpliste* mind.'

I said that Kranitski was obviously religious.

'Yes,' she said, 'but to be like that, one must be born like that.'

I said that curious explosions often happened to people. I had heard people talk of divine dynamite.

'Yes, but not to the people who want them

to happen.'

I said perhaps the method of the French priest in China was the best.

'Yes, if only one could do it – I can't.'

I said that I felt as she did about these things.

'I know so many people who are just in the same state,' she said. 'Perhaps it's like wishing to be musical when one isn't. But after all one *does* change, doesn't one?'

I said some people did, certainly. When one was in one frame of mind one couldn't imagine what it would be like to be in another.

'Yes,' she said, 'but I suppose there's a difference between being in one frame of mind and not wishing ever to be in another, and in being in the same frame of mind but longing to be in another.'

I asked if she knew how long Kranitski was going to stay at Haréville.

'Oh, I don't know,' she said, 'it all depends.'

'On his health?'

'I don't think so. He's quite well.'

'Religion must be all or nothing,' I said, going back to the topic.

'Yes, of course.'

'If I was religious I should–'

She interrupted me in the middle of my sentence.

'Mr Rudd is writing a book,' she said. 'Aunt Netty asked him what it was about, and he said it was going to be a private book, a book that he would only write in his holidays for his own amusement. She asked him whether he had begun it. He said he was only planning it, but he had got an idea. He doesn't like Mabel Summer. He thinks she is laughing at him. She isn't really, but she sees through him. I don't mean he pretends to be anything he isn't, but she sees all there is to see, and no more. He likes one to see more. Aunt Netty sees a great deal more. I see less probably. I'm unfair to him, I know. I know I'm very intolerant. You are so tolerant.'

I said I wasn't really, but kept my intolerances to myself out of policy. It was a prudent policy for one in my position.

'Mr Rudd adores you,' she said. 'He says you are so acute, so sensitive and so sensible.'

I said I was a good listener.

'Has he told you about his book?'

I said that he had told me what he had told them.

'M. Kranitski has such a funny idea about it,' she said.

I asked what the idea was.

'He thinks he is writing a book about all of us.'

'Who is the heroine?' I asked.

'Mabel – I think,' she said. 'She's so pretty. Mr Rudd admires her. He said she was like a Tanagra, and I can see she puzzles him. He's afraid of her.'

'And who is the hero?' I asked.

'I can't imagine,' she said. 'I expect he has invented one.'

'Why is the book private?'

'Because it's about real people.'

'Then we may all of us be in it?'

'Yes.'

'What made Kranitski think that?' I asked.

'The way he discusses all our characters. Each person who isn't there with all the others who are there. For instance, he discusses Princess Kouragine with Aunt Netty, and Mabel with Princess Kouragine, and you with all of us; and M. Kranitski says he talks about people like a stage-manager settling what actors must be cast for a particular play. He checks what one person tells him with what the others say. I have noticed it myself. He talked to me for hours about Mabel one day, and after he had discussed Princess Kouragine with us, he asked Mabel what she thought of her. That is to say, he told her what he thought, and then asked her if she agreed. I don't think he listened to what she said. He hardly ever listens. He talks in monologues. But there must be someone there to listen.'

'You have left out one of the characters,' I said.

'Have I?'

'The most important one.'

'The hero?'

'And the heroine.'

'He's sure to invent those.'

'I'm not so sure, I think you have left out the most important character.'

'I don't think so.'

'I mean yourself.'

'Oh no, that's nonsense; he never pays any attention to me at all. He doesn't talk about me to Aunt Netty or to the others.'

'Perhaps he has made up his mind.'

'Yes,' she said slowly, 'that's just it. He has made up his mind. He thinks I'm a – well, just a lay figure.'

I said I was certain she would not be left out if he was writing that kind of book.

She laughed happily – so happily that I imagined her looking radiant and felt that the lamp was lit. I asked her why she was laughing.

'I'm laughing,' she said, 'because in one sense my novel is over – with the ordinary happy, conventional ending – the reason I wanted to talk to you today was to tell you–'

At that moment Mrs Lennox joined us. Miss Brandon's voice passed quite naturally into another key, as she said:

'Here is Aunt Netty.'

'I have been looking for you everywhere,' said Mrs Lennox, 'I've got a headache, and we've so many letters to write. When we've done them you can watch me doing my patience.'

She said these last words as if she was conferring an undeserved reward on a truant child.

CHAPTER VIII

Later on in the evening, about six o'clock, as I was drinking a glass of water in the Pavilion, someone nearly ran into me and was saved from doing so by the intervention of a stranger who saw at once I was blind, although the other person had not noticed it. He shepherded me away from the danger and apologized. He said he supposed I was an Englishman, and that he was one too. He told me his name was Canning. We talked a little. He asked me if I was staying at the Splendide. I said I was. He said he had hoped to meet some friends of his, who he had understood were staying there too, but he could not find their names on the list of visitors. A Mrs Lennox, he said, and her niece, Miss Brandon. Did I know them? I told him they were staying at the hotel; not at the hotel proper, but at the annexe, which was a separate building. I described to him where it was. The man's voice struck me. It was so gentle, so courteous, with a tinge of melancholy in it. I asked him if he was taking the waters? He said he hadn't settled. He liked watering-places. Then our brief conversation came to an end.

After dinner, Rudd fetched me and I joined the group. I was introduced to the stranger I met in the morning: Captain Canning they called him. Mrs Summer and Princess Kouragine were sitting with them. They all talked a great deal, except Miss Brandon, who said little, and Captain Canning who said nothing.

The next morning Kranitski met me at the Pavilion, and we talked a great deal. He was in high spirits and looking forward to an expedition to the lakes which Mrs Lennox had organized. He was going with her, Miss Brandon and others. While we were sitting on a seat in the *Galeries* the postman went by with the letters. There was a letter for

Kranitski, and he asked me if I minded his reading it. He read it. There was a silence and then suddenly he laughed: a short rather mirthless chuckle. We neither of us said anything for a moment, and I felt, I knew, something had happened. There was a curious strain in his voice which seemed to come from another place, as he said: 'It is time for my douche. I shall be late. I will see you this evening.' He then left me. I saw nobody for the rest of the day.

The next day I saw some of the group in the morning just before *déjeuner*. Rudd read out a short story to us from a magazine. After luncheon Rudd came up to my room. He wished to have a talk. He had been so busy lately.

'With your book?' I asked.

'No. I have had no time to touch it,' he said. 'It's all simmering in my mind. I daresay I shall never write it at all.'

I asked him who Captain Canning was. He knew all about him. He was the young man who had once been engaged to Miss

Brandon, so Mrs Lennox had told him. But it was quite obvious that he no longer cared for her.

'Then why did he come here?' I asked.

'He caught fever in India and wanted to consult Doctor Sabran, the great malaria expert here. He was not staying on. He was going away in a few days' time. That was one reason. There was another. Donna Maria Alberti, the beautiful Italian, had been here for a night on her way to Italy. Canning had met her in Africa and was said to be devoted to her.

I asked him why he thought Canning no longer cared for Miss Brandon.

'Because,' he said, 'if he did he would propose to her at once.'

'But money,' I said.

That was all right now. His uncle had died. He was quite well off. He could marry if he wanted to. He had not paid the slightest attention to Miss Brandon.

'And she?' I asked.

'He is a different person now to what he

was, but she is the same. She accepts the fact.'

'But does she love anyone else?'

'Oh! that–'

'Is "another story"?' I said.

'Quite a different story,' he said gravely.

Rudd then left me. He was going out with Mrs Lennox. Not long after he had gone, Canning himself came and talked to me. He said he was not staying long. He had not much leave and there was a great deal he must do in England. He had come here to see a special doctor who was supposed to know all about malaria. But he had found this doctor was no longer here. He had meant to have a holiday, as he liked watering-places – they amused him – but he found he had had so much to do in England. He kept on getting so many business letters that he would have to go away much sooner than he intended. He was going back to South Africa at the end of the month.

'I have still got another year out there,' he said. 'After that I shall take up the career of a farmer in England, unless I settle in Africa altogether. It is a wonderful place. I have been so much away that I hardly feel at home in England now. At least, I think I shall hardly feel at home there. I only passed through London on my way out here.'

I told him that if he ever came to Italy he must stay with me at Cadenabbia. He said he would like to come to Italy. He had several Italian friends. One of them, Donna Maria Alberti, had been here yesterday, but she had gone. He sat for some time with me, but he did not talk much.

After dinner I found the usual group, all but Miss Brandon who had got a headache, and Kranitski who was playing in the Casino. Canning joined us for a moment, but he did not stay long.

The next day I saw nothing of any of the group. There were races going on not far off, and I had gathered that Mrs Lennox was going to these.

It was two or three days after this that Kranitski came up to my room at ten o'clock in the morning, and asked whether he could see me. He said he wanted to say 'Goodbye', as he was going away.

'My plans have been changed,' he said. 'I am going to London, and then probably to South Africa at the end of the month. I have been making the acquaintance of that nice Englishman, Canning. I am going with him.'

'Just for the sea voyage?' I asked.

'No; I shall stay there for a long time. I am *Europamüde*, if you know what that means – tired of Europe.'

'And of Russia?' I asked.

'Most of all of Russia,' he said.

'I want to tell you one thing,' he went on. 'After our meeting the other day I have been thinking you might think wrong. You are what we call in Russia very *chutki*, with a very keen scent in impressions. I want you not to misjudge. You may be thinking the obstacle has come back. It hasn't. I am free as air, as empty air. That is what I have been wanting to tell you. If you are understanding, well and good. If you are not understanding, I can tell you no more. I have enjoyed our acquaintance. We have not been knowing each other much, yet I know you very well now. I want to thank you and go.'

I asked him if he would like letters. I said I wrote letters on a typewriter.

He said he would. I told him he could write to me if he didn't mind letters being read out. My sister generally read my letters to me. She stayed with me whenever she could at Cadenabbia. But now she was busy.

He said he would write. He didn't mind who read his letters. I told him I lived all the year in Italy, and very seldom saw anyone, so that I should have little news to send him. 'Tell me what you are thinking,' he said. 'That is all the news I want.'

I asked if there was anything else I could do for him. He said, 'Yes, send me any books that Mr Rudd writes. They would interest me.'

I promised him I would do this. Then he said 'Goodbye.' He went away by the seven o'clock train.

That evening I saw no one. The next morning I learnt that Canning had gone too.

Rudd came up to my rooms to see me, but I told Henry I was not well and he did not let him come in.

The next morning I talked to Princess Kouragine at the door of the hotel. She was just leaving. I asked after Miss Brandon.

'They have gone,' said the Princess. 'They went last night to Paris. They are going to Munich and then to Bayreuth. Jean asked me to say "Goodbye" to you. She said she hopes you will come here next year.'

'Has Rudd gone with them?' I asked.

'He will meet them at Bayreuth later. He does not love Mozart. And there is a Mozart festival at Munich.'

I asked after Miss Brandon.

'The same as before,' said the Princess. 'The lamp was lit for a moment, but they put it out. It is a pity. The man behaved well.'

At that moment we were interrupted. I wanted to ask her a great deal more. But the motor bus drove up to the door. She said

'Goodbye' to me. She was going to Paris. She would spend the winter at Rome.

In the afternoon I saw Mrs Summer, but only for a moment. She told me Miss Brandon had sent me a lot of messages, and I wanted to ask her what had happened and how things stood, but she had an engagement. We arranged to meet and have a long talk the next morning.

But when the next morning came, I got a message from her, saying she had been obliged to go to London at once to meet her husband.

A little later in the day, I received a letter by post from my unmarried sister, saying she would meet me in Paris and we could both go back to Italy together. So I decided to do this. I saw Rudd once before I left. He dined with me on my last night. He said that his holiday was shortly coming to an end. He would spend three days at Bayreuth and then he would go back to work.

'On the Sleeping Beauty?' I asked.

'No, not on that.' He doubted whether he

would ever touch that again. The idea of it had been only a holiday amusement at first. 'But now,' he said, 'the idea has grown. If I do it, it will have to be a real book, even if only a short one, a *nouvelle*. The idea is a fascinating one. The Sleeping Beauty awake and changed in an alien world. Perhaps I may do it some day. If I do, I will send it to you. In any case I was right about Miss Brandon. She would be a better heroine for a fairy tale than for a modern story. She is too emotionless, too calm for a modern novel.'

'I have got another idea,' he went on, 'I am thinking of writing a story about a woman who looked as delicate as a flower, and who crushed those who came into contact with her and destroyed those who loved her. The idea is only a shadow as yet. But it may come to something. In any case I must do some regular work at once. I have had a long enough holiday. I have been wasting my time. I have enjoyed it, it has done me good, and conversations are never wasted, as they are the breeding ground of ideas. Sometimes the ideas do not flower for years. But the seed is sown in talk. I am grateful to you too, and I hope I shall meet you here again next year. I can't invent anything unless I am in sympathetic surroundings.'

The next day I left Haréville and met my sister in Paris. We travelled to Cadenabbia together.

PART TWO

FROM THE PAPERS OF
ANTHONY KAY

CHAPTER I

Two years after I had written these few chapters, I was sent once more to Haréville. Again I went early in the season. There was nobody left of the old group I had known during my first visit. Mrs Lennox and her niece were not there, and they were not expected. They had spent some months at Haréville the preceding year.

I had spent the intervening time in Italy. I had heard once or twice from Mrs Summer, and sometimes from Kranitski. He had gone to South Africa with Canning and had stayed there. He liked the country. Miss Brandon was not yet married. Princess Kouragine I had not seen again. Rudd I had neither heard from nor of. Apparently he had published one book since he had been to Haréville and several short stories in magazines. The book was called *The Silver Sandal,* and had nothing to do with any of his experiences here or with any of the fancies which they had called up. It was, on the contrary, a semi-historical romance of a fantastic nature.

During the first days of my stay here I made no acquaintances, and I was already counting on a dreary three weeks of unrelieved dullness when my doctor here introduced me to Sabran, the malaria specialist, who had been away during my first cure.

Dr Sabran, besides being a specialist with a reverberating reputation and a widely travelled man of great experience and European culture, had a different side to his nature which was not even suspected by many of his patients.

Under the pseudonym of Gaspard Lautrec he had written some charming stories and some interesting studies in art and literature. Historical questions interested him; and still more, the quainter facts of human nature, psychological puzzles, mysterious episodes, unvisited byways, and baffling and unsolved problems in history, romance and everyday life. He was a voracious reader, and there was little that had escaped his notice in the contemporary literature of Europe.

I found him an extraordinarily interesting companion, and he was kind enough, busy as I knew him to be, either to come and see me daily, or to invite me to his house. I often dined with him, and we would remain talking in his sitting-room till late in the night, while he would tell me of some of the remarkable things that had come under his notice or sometimes weave startling and paradoxical theories about nature and man.

I asked him one day if he knew Rudd's work. He said he admired it, but it had always struck him as strange that a writer could be as intelligent as Rudd and yet, at the same time, so obviously *à côté* with regard to some of the more important springs and factors of human nature.

I asked him what made him think that.

'All his books,' he said, 'any of them. I have just been reading his last book in the Tauchnitz edition, a book of stories, not short stories: *nouvelles*. It is called *Unfinished Dramas*. I will lend it you if you like.'

We talked of other things, and I took the book away with me when I went away. The next day I received a letter from Rudd, sending me a privately printed story (one of 500 signed copies) called *Overlooked*, which, he said, completed the series of his Unfinished Dramas, but which he had not published for reasons which I would understand.

Henry read out Rudd's new book to me. There were three stories in the book. They did not interest me greatly, and I made Henry hurry through them; but the privately printed story *Overlooked* was none other than the story he had thought of writing when we were at Haréville together.

He had written the story more or less as he had said he had intended to. All the characters of our old group were in it. Miss

Brandon was the centre, and Kranitski appeared, not as a Swede but as a Russian. I myself flitted across the scene for a moment.

The facts which he related were as far as I knew actually those which had occurred to that group of people during their stay at Haréville two years ago, but the deductions he drew from them, the causes he gave as explaining them, seemed to me at least wide of the mark.

His conception of such of his characters as I knew at all well, and his interpretation of their motives were, in the cases in which I had the power of checking them by my own experience, I considered quite fantastically wrong.

When I had finished reading the book, I sent it to Sabran, and with it the MS I had written two years ago, and I begged the doctor to read what I had written and to let me know when he had done so, so that we might discuss both the documents and their relation one to the other and to the reality.

(Note – Here, in the bound copy of Anthony Kay's Papers, follows the story called *Overlooked,* by James Rudd.)

OVERLOOKED

By James Rudd

1

It was the after-luncheon hour at Saint-Yves-les-Bains. The Pavilion, with its large tepid glass dome and polished brass fountains, where the salutary, and somewhat steely, waters flowed unceasingly, the Pompeian pillared *Galeries* were deserted; so were the trim park with its kiosk, where a scanty orchestra played ragtime in the morning and in the evenings; the florid Casino, which denoted the third of the three styles of architecture that distinguished the appendages of the Hotel de La Source, where a dignified, shabby, white Louis-

Philippe nucleus was still to be detected half-concealed and altogether overwhelmed by the elegant improvements and dainty enlargements of the Second Empire and the overripe art nouveau excrescences of a later period.

Kathleen Farrel had the park to herself. She was reading the *Morning Post*, which her aunt, Mrs Knolles, took in for the literary articles, and which you would find on her table side by side with newspapers and journals of a widely different and some-times, indeed, of a startling and flamboyant character; for Mrs Knolles was catholic in her ideas and daring in her tastes.

Kathleen Farrel was reading listlessly without interest. She had lived so much abroad that English news had little attrac-tion for her, and she was no longer young enough to regret missing any of the recep-tions, race meetings, garden-parties, and other social events which she was idly skim-ming the record of. For it was now the height of the London season, but Mrs

Knolles had let the London house in Hill Street. She always let it every summer, and in the winter as well, whenever she could find a tenant.

A paragraph had caught Kathleen's eye and had arrested her attention. It began thus: 'The death has occurred at Monkswell Hall of Sir James Stukely.'

Sir James Stukely was Lancelot Stukely's uncle. Lancelot would inherit the baronetcy and a comfortable income. He had left the Army some years ago. He was at present abroad, performing some kind of secretarial duties to the Governor of Malta. He would give up that job, which was neither lucrative nor interesting, he would come home, and then–

At any rate, he had not altogether forgotten her. His monthly letters proved that. They had been unfailingly regular. Only – well, for the last year they had been undefinably different. Ever since that visit to Cairo. She had heard stories of an attachment, a handsome Italian lady, who looked like a Renaissance picture and who was said to be unscrupulous. But she really knew nothing, and Lancelot had always been so reserved, so reticent; his letters had always been so bald, almost formal, ever since their brief engagement six years before had been broken off. Ever since that memorable night in Ireland when she confessed to her father, who was more than usually violent and had drunk an extra glass of old Madeira, that she had refused to marry Lancelot. At first she had asked him not to write, and he had dutifully accepted the restriction. But later, when her father died, he had written to her and she had answered his letter. Since then he had written once a month without fail from India, where his regiment had been quartered, and then from Malta. But never had there been a single allusion to the past or to the future. The tone of them would be: 'Dear Miss Farrel, We are having very good sport.' Or 'Dear Miss Farrel, We went to the opera last night. It was too classical for me.' And they had always ended: 'Yours sincerely,

Lancelot Stukely.'

And yet she could not believe he was really different. Was she different? 'Am I perhaps different?' she thought. She dismissed the idea. What had happened to make her different? Nothing. For the last five years, ever since her father had died, she had lived the same life. The winter at her aunt's villa at Bordighera, sometimes a week or two at Florence, the summer at Saint-Yves-les-Bains, where they lived in the hotel, on special terms, as Mrs Knolles was such a constant client. Never a new note, always the same gang of people round them; the fashionable cosmopolitan world of continental watering-places, the English and foreign colonies of the Riviera and North Italy. She had never met anyone who had roused her interest, and the only persons whose attention she had seemed to attract were, in her Aunt Elsie's words, 'frankly impossible'.

She would be thirty next year. She already felt infinitely older. 'But perhaps,' she thought, 'he will come back the same as he was before. He will propose and I will accept him this time.' Why had she refused him? Their financial situation – her poverty and his own very small income had had nothing to do with it, because Lancelot had said he was willing to wait for years, and everyone knew he had expectations. She could not have left her father, but then her father died a year after she refused Lancelot.

No, the reason had been that she thought she did not love him. She had liked Lancelot, but she hoped for something more and something different. A fairy prince who would wake her to a different life. As soon as he had gone away, and still more when his series of formal letters began, she realized that she had made a mistake, and she had never ceased to repent her action. The fact was, she said to herself, I was too young to make such a decision. I did not know my own mind. If only he had come back when father died. If only he had been a little more insistent. He had accepted everything without a murmur. And yet now she felt certain he had been faithful and was faithful still, whatever anyone might say to the contrary.

'Perhaps I am altered,' she thought. 'Perhaps he won't even recognize me.' And yet she knew she did not believe this. For although her Aunt Elsie used to be seriously anxious about her niece's looks – fearing anaemia, so much so that they sometimes visited dreary places on the sea-coasts of England and France – she knew her looks had not altered sensibly. People still stared at her when she entered a room, for although there was nothing classical nor brilliant about her features and her appearance, hers was a face you could not fail to observe and which it was difficult to forget. It was a face that appealed to artists. They would have liked to try and paint that clear white, delicate skin, and those extraordinarily haunting round eyes which looked violet in some lights and a deep sea blue in others, and to try and render the romantic childish glamour of her person, that wistful, fairy-tale-like expression. It was extraordinary that with such an appearance she should have been the inspirer of no romance, but so it was. Painters had admired her; one or two adventurers had proposed to her; but with the exception of Lancelot Stukely no one had fallen in love with her. Perhaps she had frightened people. She could not make conversation. She did not care for books. She knew nothing of art, and the people her aunt saw – most of whom were foreigners – talked glibly and sometimes wittily of all these things.

Kathleen had been born for a country life, and she was condemned to live in cities and in watering-places. She was insular; though she had lived a great deal in Ireland, she was not Irish, and she had been cast for a continental part. She was matter-of-fact, and her appearance promised the opposite. She was in a sense the victim of her looks, which were so misleading.

But perhaps the solution, the real solution of the absence of romance, or even of suitors, was to be found in her unconquerable listlessness and apathy. She was, as it were, only half-alive.

Once, when she was a little girl, she had gone to pick flowers in the great dark wood near her home, where the trees had huge fantastic trunks, and gnarled boles, and where in the springtime the bluebells stretched beneath them like an unbroken blue sea. After she had been picking bluebells for nearly an hour, she had felt sleepy. She lay down under the trunk of a tree. A gypsy passed her and asked to tell her fortune. She had waved her away, as she had no sympathy with gypsies. The gypsy had said that she would give her a piece of good advice unasked, and that was, not to go to sleep in the forest on the Eve of St John, for if she did she would never wake. She paid no attention to this, and she dozed off to sleep and slept for about half an hour. She was an obstinate child, and not at all superstitious. When she got home, she asked the housekeeper when was the Eve of St John. It happened to fall on that very day. She said to herself that this proved what nonsense the gypsies talked, as she had slept, woken up, come back to the house, and had high tea in the schoolroom as usual. She never gave the incident another thought; but the house-keeper, who was superstitious, told one of the maids that Miss Kathleen had been over-looked by the fairy folk and would never be quite the same again. When she was asked for further explanations, she would not give any. But to all outward appearances Kathleen was the same, and nobody noticed any difference in her, nor did she feel that she had suffered any change.

As long as she had lived with her father in Ireland, she had been fairly lively. She had enjoyed outdoor life. The house, a ram-shackle, Georgian grey building, was near the sea, and her father who had been a sailor used sometimes to take her out sailing. She had ridden and sometimes hunted. All this she had enjoyed. It was only after she dis-missed Lancelot, who had known her ever since she was sixteen, that the mist of apathy had descended on her. After her father's death, this mist had increased in thickness, and when her continental life with her aunt had begun, she had altogether lost any particle of *joie de vivre* she had ever had. Nor did she seem to notice it or to regret the past. She never complained. She accepted her aunt's plans and decisions, and never made any objection, never even a suggestion or a comment.

Her aunt was truly fond of her, and she tried to devise treats to please her, and tried to awaken her interest in things. One year she had taken Kathleen to Bayreuth, hoping to rouse her interest in music, but Kathleen had found the music tedious and noisy, although she listened to it without complaining, and when her aunt suggested going there another year, she agreed to the suggestion with alacrity. The only thing which ever roused her interest was horse-racing. Sometimes they went to the races near Saint-Yves, and then Kathleen would become a different girl. She would be, as long as the racing lasted, alive for the time being, and sink back into her dreamless apathy as soon as they were over.

At the same time, whenever she thought of Lancelot Stukely she felt a pang of regret, and after reading this paragraph in the *Morning Post*, she hoped, more than ever she had hoped before, that he would come back, and come back unchanged and faithful, and that she would be the same for him as she had been before, and that she would once more be able to make his slow honest eyes light up and smoulder with love, admiration and passion.

'This time I will not make the same mistake,' she said to herself. 'If he gives me the chance—'

2

Her reverie was interrupted by the approach of an hotel acquaintance. It was Anikin, the Russian, who had in the last month become an accepted and established factor in their small group of hotel acquaintances. Kathleen had met him first some years ago at Rome, but it was only at Saint-Yves that she had come to know him.

As he took off his hat in a hesitating manner, as if afraid of interrupting her thoughts, she registered the fact that she knew him, not only better than anyone else at the hotel, but better almost than anyone anywhere.

'Would you like a game?' he asked. He meant a game which was provided in the park for the distraction of the patients. It consisted in throwing a small ring, attached to a post by a string, on to hooks which were fixed on an upright sloping board. The hooks had numbers underneath them, which varied from one to 5,000.

'Not just at present,' she said, 'I am waiting for Aunt Elsie. I must see what she is going to do, but later on I should love a game.'

He smiled and went on. He understood that she wanted to be left alone. He had that swift, unerring comprehension of the small and superficial shades of the mind, the minor feelings, social values, and human relations that so often distinguishes his countrymen.

He might, indeed, have stepped out of a Russian novel, with his untidy hair, his short-sighted, kindly eyes, his colourless skin, and nondescript clothes. Kathleen had never reflected before whether she liked him or disliked him. She had accepted him as part of the place, and she had not noticed the easiness of relations with him. It came upon her now with a slight shock that these relations were almost peculiar from their ease and naturalness. It was as if she had known him for years, whereas she had not known him for more than a month. All this flashed through her mind, which then went back to the paragraph in the *Morning Post*, when her aunt rustled up to her.

Mrs Knolles had the supreme elegance of being smart without looking conventional, as if she led rather than followed the fashion. There was always something personal and individual about her Parisian hats, her jewels, and her cloaks; and there was something rich, daring and exotic about her sumptuous sombre hair, with its sudden gold-copper glints and her soft brown eyes. There was nothing apathetic about her. She was filled to the brim with life, with interest, with energy. She cast a glance at the *Morning Post*, and said rather impatiently:

'My dear child, what are you reading? That newspaper is ten days old. Don't you see it is dated the first?'

'So it is,' said Kathleen apologetically. But that moment a thought flashed through her: 'Then, surely, Lancelot must be on his way home, if he is not back already.'

'I've brought you your letters,' said her aunt. 'Here they are.'

Kathleen reached for them more eagerly than usual. She expected to see, she hoped, at least, to see, Lancelot's rather childish handwriting, but both the letters were bills.

'Mr Arkright and Anikin are dining with us,' said her aunt, 'and Count Tilsit.'

Kathleen said nothing.

'You don't mind?' said her aunt.

'Of course not.'

'I thought you liked Count Tilsit.'

'Oh, yes, I do,' said Kathleen.

Kathleen felt that she had, against her intention, expressed disappointment, or rather that she had not expressed the necessary blend of surprise and pleasure. But as Arkright and Anikin dined with them frequently, and as she had forgotten who Count Tilsit was, this was difficult for her. Arkright was an English author, who was a friend of her aunt's, and had sufficient penetration to realize that Mrs Knolles was something more than a woman of the world; to appreciate her fundamental goodness as well as her obvious cleverness, and to divine that Kathleen's exterior might be in some ways deceptive.

'You remember him in Florence?' said Mrs Knolles, reverting to Count Tilsit.

'Oh, yes, the Norwegian.'

'A Swede, darling, not a Norwegian.'

'I thought it was the same thing,' said Kathleen.

'I have got a piece of news for you,' said Mrs Knolles.

Kathleen made an effort to prepare her face. She was determined that it should reveal nothing. She knew quite well what was coming.

'Lancelot Stukely is in London,' her aunt went on. 'He came back just in time to see his uncle before he died. His uncle has left him everything.'

'Was Sir James ill a long time?' Kathleen asked.

'I believe he was,' said Mrs Knolles.

'Oh, then I suppose he won't go back to Malta,' said Kathleen, with perfectly assumed indifference.

'Of course not,' said Mrs Knolles. 'He inherits the place, the title, everything. He will be very well off. Would you like to drive to Batigny this afternoon? Princess Oulchikov can take us in her motor if you would like to go. Arkright is coming.'

'I will if you want me to,' said Kathleen.

This was one of the remarks that Kathleen

often made, which annoyed her aunt, and perhaps justly. Mrs Knolles was always trying to devise something that would amuse or distract her niece, but whenever she suggested anything to her or arranged any expedition or special treat which she thought might amuse, all the response she met with was a phrase that implied resignation.

'I don't want you to come if you would rather not,' she said with beautifully concealed impatience.

'Well, today I *would* rather not,' said Kathleen, greatly to her aunt's surprise. It was the first time she had ever made such an answer.

'Aren't you feeling well, darling?' she asked gently.

'Quite well, Aunt Elsie, I promise,' Kathleen said smiling, 'but I said I would sit and talk to Mr Asham this afternoon.'

Mr Asham was a blind man who had been ordered to take the waters at Saint-Yves. Kathleen had made friends with him.

'Very well,' said Mrs Knolles, with a sigh.

'I must go. The motor will be there. Don't forget we've got people dining with us tonight, and don't wear your grey. It's too shabby.' One of Miss Farrel's practices, which irritated her aunt, was to wear her shabbiest clothes on an occasion that called for dress, and to take pains, as it were, not to do herself justice.

Her aunt left her.

Kathleen had made no arrangement with Asham. She had invented the excuse on the spur of the moment, but she knew he would be in the park in the afternoon. She wanted to think. She wanted to be alone. If Lancelot had been in England when Sir James died, then he must have started home at least a fortnight ago, as the news that she had read was ten days old. She had not heard from him for over a month. This meant that his uncle had been ill, he had returned to London, and had experienced a change of fortune without writing her one word.

'All the same,' she thought, 'it proves nothing.'

At that moment a friendly voice called to her.

'What are you doing all by yourself, Kathleen?'

It was her friend, Mrs Roseleigh. Kathleen had known Eva Roseleigh all her life, although her friend was ten years older than herself and was married. She was staying at Saint-Yves by herself. Her husband was engrossed in other occupations and complications besides those of his business in the city, and of a different nature. Mrs Roseleigh was one of those women whom her friends talked of with pity, saying 'Poor Eva'! But 'Poor Eva' had a large income, a comfortable house in Upper Brook Street. She was slight, and elegant; as graceful as a Tanagra figure, fair, delicate-looking, appealing and plaintive to look at, with sympathetic grey eyes. Her husband was a successful man of business, and some people said that the neglect he showed his wife and the publicity of his infidelities was not to be wondered at, considering the contempt with which she treated him. It was more a case of 'Poor Charlie', they said, than 'Poor Eva'.

Kathleen would not have agreed with these opinions. She was never tired of saying that Eva was 'wonderful'. She was certainly a good friend to Kathleen.

'Sir James Stukely is dead,' said Kathleen.

'I saw that in the newspaper some time ago. I thought you knew,' said Mrs Roseleigh.

'It was stupid of me not to know. I read the newspapers so seldom and so badly.'

'That means Lancelot will come home.'

'He has come home.'

'Oh, you know then?'

'Know what?'

'That he is coming here?'

Kathleen blushed crimson. 'Coming here! How do you know?'

'I saw his name,' said Mrs Roseleigh, 'on the board in the hall of the hotel, and I asked if he had arrived. They told me they were expecting him tonight.'

At that moment a tall dark lady, elegant as

a figure carved by Jean Goujon, and splendid as a Titian, no longer young, but still more than beautiful, walked past them, talking rather vehemently in Italian to a young man, also an Italian.

'Who is that?' asked Kathleen.

'That,' said Mrs Roseleigh, 'is Donna Laura Bartolini. She is still very beautiful, isn't she? The man with her is a diplomat.'

'I think,' said Kathleen, 'she is very striking looking. But what extraordinary clothes.'

'They are specially designed for her.'

'Do you know her?'

'A little. She is not at all what she seems to be. She is, at heart, matter-of-fact, and domestic, but she dresses like a Bacchante. She has still many devoted adorers.'

'Here?'

'Everywhere. But she worships her husband.'

'Is he here?'

'No, but I think he is coming.'

'I remember hearing about her a long time ago. I think she was at Cairo once.'

'Very likely. Her husband is an archae-ologist, a savant.'

Was that the woman, thought Kathleen, to whom Lancelot was supposed to have been devoted? If so, it wasn't true. She was sure it wasn't true. Lancelot would never have been attracted by that type of woman, and yet—

'Aunt Elsie has asked a Swede to dinner. Count Tilsit. Do you know him?'

'I was introduced to him yesterday. He admired you.'

'Do you like him?'

'I hardly know him. I think he is nice-looking and has good manners and looks like an Englishman.'

But Kathleen was no longer listening. She was thinking of Lancelot, of his sudden arrival. What could it mean? Did he know they were here? The last time he had written was a month ago from London. Had she said they were coming here? She thought she had. Perhaps she had not. In any case that would hardly make any difference, as he knew they went abroad every year, knew they went to Saint-Yves most years, and if he didn't know, would surely hear it in London. Yes, he must know. Then it meant either that – or perhaps it meant something quite different. Perhaps the doctor had sent him to Saint-Yves. He had suffered from attacks of Malta fever several times. Saint-Yves was good for malaria. There was a well-known malaria specialist on the medical staff. He might be coming to consult him. What did she want to be the truth? What did she feel? She scarcely knew herself. She felt exhilarated, as if life had suddenly become different, more interesting and strangely iridescent. What would Lancelot be like? Would he be the same? Or would he be someone quite different? She couldn't talk about it, not even to Eva, although Eva had known all about it, and Mrs Roseleigh with her acute intuition guessed that, and guessed what Kathleen was thinking about, and said nothing that fringed the topic; but what disconcerted Kathleen and gave her a slight quiver of alarm was that she thought she discerned in Eva's voice and manner the faintest note of pity; she experienced an almost imperceptible chill in the temperature; an inkling, the ghost of a warning, as if Eva were thinking, 'You mustn't be disappointed if–' Well, she wouldn't be disappointed *if.* At least nobody should divine her disappointment: not even Eva.

Mrs Roseleigh guessed that her friend wanted to be alone and left her on some quickly invented pretext. As soon as she was alone Kathleen rose from her seat and went for a walk by herself beyond the park and through the village. Then she came back and played a game with Anikin at the ring board, and at five o'clock she had a talk with Asham to quiet her conscience. She stayed out late, until, in fact, the motor bus, which met the evening express, arrived from the station at seven o'clock. She watched its arrival from a distance, from the galleries, while she simulated interest in the shop windows. But as the motor bus was emptied of its passengers, she caught no sight of Lancelot. When the omnibus had gone, and the new arrivals left the scene, she walked into the hall of the hotel, and asked the porter whether many new visitors had arrived.

'Two English gentlemen,' he said, 'Lord Frimhurst and Sir Lancelot Stukely.' She ran upstairs to dress for dinner, and even her Aunt Elsie was satisfied with her appearance that night. She had put on her sea-green tea gown: a present from Eva, made in Paris.

'I wish you always dressed like that,' said Mrs Knolles, as they walked into the Casino dining-room. 'You can't think what a difference it makes. It's so foolish not to make the best of oneself when it needs so very little trouble.' But Mrs Knolles had the untaught and unlearnable gift of looking her best at any season, at any hour. It was, indeed, no trouble to her; but all the trouble in the world could not help others to achieve the effects which seemed to come to her by accident.

As they walked into the large hotel dining-room, Kathleen was conscious that everyone was looking at her, except Lancelot, if he was there, and she felt he *was* there. Arkright and Count Tilsit were waiting for them at their table and stood up as they walked in. They were followed almost immediately by Princess Oulchikov, whose French origin and education were made manifest by her mauve chiffon shawl, her buckled shoes, and the tortoiseshell comb in her glossy black hair. Nothing could have been more unpretentious than her clothes, and nothing more common to hundreds of her kind, than her single row of pearls and her little platinum wristwatch, but the manner in which she wore these things was French, as clearly and unmistakably French and not Russian, Italian, or English, as an article signed Jules Lemaître or the ribbons of a chocolate Easter egg from the Passage des Panoramas. She looked like a Winterhalter portrait of a lady who had been a great beauty in the days of the Second Empire.

Her married life with Prince Oulchikov, once a brilliant and reckless cavalry officer, and not long ago deceased, after many vicissitudes of fortune, ending by prosperity, since he had died too soon after inheriting a third fortune to squander it, as he had managed to squander two former inheritances, and her at one time prolonged sojourns in the country of her adoption had left no trace on her appearance. As to their effect on her soul and mind, that was another and an altogether different question.

Mrs Knolles, whose harmonious draperies of black and yellow seemed to call for the brush of a daring painter, sat at the further end of the table next to the window, on her left at the end of the table Arkright, whom you would never have taken for an author, since his motto was what a Frenchman once said to a young painter who affected long hair and eccentric clothes: *'Ne savez-vous pas qu'il faut s'habiller comme tout le monde et peindre comme personne?'* On his other side sat Princess Oulchikov; next to her at the end of the table, Kathleen, and then Count Tilsit (fair, blue-eyed, and shy) on Mrs Knolles's right.

Kathleen, being at the end of the table, could not see any of the tables behind her, but in front of her was a gilded mirror, and no sooner had they sat down to dinner than she was aware, in this glass, of the reflection of Lancelot Stukely's back, who was sitting at a table with a party of people just opposite to them on the other side of the room. There was nothing more remarkable about Lancelot Stukely's front view than about his back view, and that, in spite of a certain military squareness of shoulder, had a slight stoop. He was small and seemed made to grace the front windows of a club in St James's Street; everything about him was correct, and his face had the honest refinement of a well-bred dog that has been admirably trained and only barks at the right kind of stranger.

But the sudden sight of Lancelot transformed Kathleen. It was as if someone had lit a lamp behind her alabaster mask, and in the effort to conceal any embarrassment, or preoccupation, she flushed and became unusually lively and talked to Anikin with a gaiety and an uninterrupted ease, that seemed not to belong to her usual self.

And yet, while she talked, she found time every now and then to study the reflections of the mirror in front of them, and these told her that Lancelot was sitting next to Donna Laura Bartolini. The young man she had seen talking to Donna Laura was there also. There were others whom she did not know.

Mrs Knolles was busily engaged in thawing the stiff coating of ice of Count Tilsit's shyness, and very soon she succeeded in putting him completely at his ease; and Arkright was trying to interest Princess Oulchikov in Japanese art. But the Princess had lived too long in Russia not to catch the Slav microbe of indifference, and she was a woman who only lived by half-hours. This half-hour was one of her moment of eclipse, and she paid little attention to what Arkright said. He, however, was habituated to her ways and went on talking.

Mrs Knolles was surprised and pleased at her niece's behaviour. Never had she seen her so lively, so gay.

'Miss Farrel is looking extraordinarily well tonight,' Arkright said, in an undertone, to the Princess.

'Yes,' said Princess Oulchikov, 'she is at last taking waters from the right source.' She often made cryptic remarks of this kind, and Arkright was puzzled, for Kathleen never took the waters, but he knew the Princess well enough not to ask her to explain. Princess Oulchikov made no further comment. Her mind had already relapsed into the land of listless limbo which it loved to haunt.

Presently the conversation became general. They discussed the races, the troupe at the Casino Theatre, the latest arrivals.

'Lancelot Stukely is here,' said Mrs Knolles.

'Yes,' said Kathleen, with great calm, 'dining with Donna Laura Bartolini.'

'Oh, Laura's arrived,' said Mrs Knolles. 'I am glad. That is good news. What fun we shall all have together. Yes. There she is, looking lovely. Don't you think she's lovely?' she said to Arkright and the Princess.

Arkright admired Donna Laura unreservedly. Princess Oulchikov said she would no doubt think the same if she hadn't known her thirty years ago, and then 'those clothes,' she said, 'don't suit her, they make her look like an *art nouveau* poster.' Anikin said he did not admire her at all, and as for the clothes, she was the last person who should dare those kind of clothes; her beauty was conventional, she was made for less fantastic fashions. He looked at Kathleen. He was thinking that her type of beauty could have supported any costume, however extravagant; in fact he longed to see her draped in shimmering silver and faded gold, with strange stones in her hair. Count Tilsit, who was younger than anyone present, said he found her young.

'She is older than you think,' said Princess Oulchikov. 'I remember her coming out in Rome in 1879.'

'Do you think she is over fifty?' said Kathleen.

'I do not think it, I am sure,' said the Princess.

'Her figure is wonderful,' said Mrs Knolles.

'Was she very beautiful then?' asked Anikin.

'The most beautiful woman I have ever seen,' said the Princess. 'People stood on chairs to look at her one night at the French Embassy. It is cruel to see her dressed as she is now.'

Count Tilsit opened his clear, round, blue eyes, and stared first at the Princess and then at Donna Laura. It was inconceivable to his young Scandinavian mind that this radiant and dazzling creature, dressed up like the queen in a Russian ballet, could be over fifty.

'To me, she has always looked exactly the same,' said Arkright. 'In fact, I admire her more now than I did when I first knew her fifteen years ago.'

'That is because you look at her with the eyes of the past,' said the Princess, 'but not of a long enough past, as I do. When you first saw her you were young, but when I first saw her *she* was young. That makes all the difference.'

'I think she is very beautiful now,' said Mrs Knolles.

'And so do I,' said Kathleen. 'I could understand anyone being in love with her.'

'That there will always be people in love with her,' said the Princess, 'and young people. She has charm as well as beauty, and how rare that is!'

'Yes,' said Anikin, pensively, 'how rare that is.'

Kathleen looked at the mirror as if she was appraising Donna Laura's beauty, but in reality it was to see whether Lancelot was talking to her. As far as she could see he seemed to be rather silent. General conversation, with a lot of Italian intermixed with it, was going up from the table like fireworks. Kathleen turned to Count Tilsit and made conversation to him, while Anikin and the Princess began to talk in a passionately argumentative manner of all the beauties they had known. The Princess had come to life once more. Mrs Knolles, having done her duty, relapsed into a comfortable conversation with Arkright. They understood each other without effort.

The Italian party finished their dinner first, and went out on to the terrace, and as they walked out of the room the extraordinary dignity of Donna Laura's carriage struck the whole room. Whatever anyone might think of her looks now, there was no doubt that her presence still carried with it the authority that only great beauty, however much it may be lessened by time, confers.

'*Elle est encore très belle,*' said Princess

Oulchikov, voicing the thoughts of the whole party.

Mrs Knolles suggested going out. Shawls were fetched and coffee was served just outside the hotel on a stone terrace.

Soon after they had sat down, Lancelot Stukely walked up to them. He was not much changed, Kathleen thought. A little grey about the temples, a little bit thinner, and slightly more tanned – his face had been burnt in the tropics – but the slow, honest eyes were the same. He said how-do-you-do to Mrs Knolles and to herself, and was presented to the others.

Mrs Knolles asked him to sit down.

'I must go back presently,' he said, 'but may I stay a minute?'

He sat down next to Kathleen.

They talked a little with pauses in between their remarks. She did not ask him how long he was going to stay, but he explained his arrival. He had come to consult the malaria specialist.

'We have all been discussing Donna Laura

Bartolini,' said Mrs Knolles. 'You were dining with her?'

'Yes,' he said, 'she is an old friend of mine.
I met her first at Cairo.'

'Is she going to stay long?' asked Mrs
Knolles.

'No,' he said, 'she is only passing through
on her way to Italy. She leaves for Ravenna
tomorrow morning.'

'She is looking beautiful,' said Mrs
Knolles.

'Yes,' he said, 'she is very beautiful, isn't
she?'

Then he got up.

'I hope we shall meet again tomorrow,' he
said to Kathleen and to Mrs Knolles.

'Are you staying on?' asked Mrs Knolles.

'Oh, no,' he said. 'I only wanted to see the
doctor. I have got to go back to England at
once. I have got so much business to do.'

'Of course,' said Mrs Knolles. 'We will see
you tomorrow. Will you come to the lakes
with us?'

Lancelot hesitated and then said that he,

alas, would be busy all day tomorrow. He had an appointment with the doctor – he had so little time.

He was slightly confused in his explanations. He then said good night, and went back to his party. They were sitting at a table under the trees.

Kathleen felt relieved, unaccountably relieved, that he had gone, and she experienced a strange exhilaration. It was as if a curtain had been lifted up and she suddenly saw a different and a new world. She had the feeling of seeing clearly for the first time for many years. She saw quite plainly that as far as Lancelot was concerned, the past was completely forgotten. She meant nothing to him at all. He was the same Lancelot, but he belonged to a different world. There were gulfs and gulfs between them now. He had come here to see Donna Laura for a few hours. He had not minded doing this, although he knew that he would meet Kathleen. He had told her himself that he knew he would meet her. He had mentioned the rarity of his letters lately. He had been so busy, and then all that business ... his uncle's death.

The situation was quite simple and quite clear. But the strange thing was that, instead of feeling her life was over, as she had expected to feel, she felt it was, on the contrary, for the first time beginning.

'I have been waiting for years,' she thought to herself, 'for this Fairy Prince, and now I see that he was not the Fairy Prince, after all. But this does not mean I may not meet the Fairy Prince, the *real* one,' and her eyes glistened.

She had never felt more alive, more ready for adventure. Anikin suggested that they should all walk in the garden. It was still daylight. They got up. The Princess, Arkright, Mrs Knolles, and Count Tilsit walked down the steps first, and passed on down an avenue.

Kathleen delayed until the others walked on some way, and then she said to Anikin, who was waiting for her:

'Let us stay and talk here. It is quieter. We can go for a walk presently.'

4

They did not stay long on the terrace. As soon as they saw which direction the rest of the party had taken they took another. They walked through the hotel gates across the street as far as a gate over which 'Bellevue' was written. They had never been there before. It was an annexe of the hotel, a kind of detached park. They climbed up the hill and passed two deserted and unused lawn tennis-courts and a dusty track once used for skittles, and emerged from a screen of thick trees on to a little plateau. Behind them was a row of trees and a green cornfield, beneath them a steep slope of grass. They could see the red roofs of the village, the roofs of the hotels, the grey spire of the village church, the park, the green plain and, in the distance rising out of the green corn, a large flat-topped hill. The long summer daylight was at last fading away. The sky was lustrous and the air was quite still.

The fields and the trees had that peculiar deep green they take on in the twilight, as if they had been dyed by the tints of the evening. Anikin said it reminded him of Russia.

Kathleen had wrapped a thin white shawl round her, and in the dimness of the hour she looked as white as a ghost, but in the pallor of her face her eyes shone like black diamonds. Anikin had never seen her look like that. And then it came to him that this was the moment of moments. Perhaps the moon had risen. The cloudless sky seemed all of a sudden to be silvered with a new light. There was a dry smell of sun-baked roads and of summer in the air, and no sound at all.

They had sat down on the bench and Kathleen was looking straight in front of her out into the west, where the last remains of the sunset had faded some time ago.

This Anikin felt was the sacred minute;

the moment of fate; the imperishable instant which Faust had asked for even at the price of his soul, but which mortal love had always denied him. In a whisper he asked Kathleen to be his wife. She got up from the seat and said very slowly:

'Yes, I will marry you.'

The words seemed to be spoken for her by something in her that was not herself, and yet she was willing that they should be spoken. She seemed to want all this to happen, and yet she felt that it was being done for her, not of her own accord, but by someone else. Her eyes shone like stars. But as he touched her hand, she still felt that she was being moved by some alien spirit separate from herself and that it was not she herself that was giving herself to him. She was obeying some exterior and foreign control which came neither from him nor from her – some mysterious outside influence. She seemed to be looking on at herself as she was whirled over the edge of a planet, but she was not making the effort, nor was it

Anikin's words, nor his look, nor his touch, that were moving her. He had taken her in his arms, and as he kissed her they heard footsteps on the path coming towards them. The spell was broken, and they gently moved apart one from the other. It was he who said quietly:

'We had better go home.'

Some French people appeared through the trees round the corner. A middle-aged man in a nankin jacket, his wife, his two little girls. They were acquaintances of Anikin and of Kathleen. It was the man who kept a haberdasher's shop in the *Galeries*. Brief mutual salutations passed and a few civilities were bandied, and then Kathleen and Anikin walked slowly down the hill in silence. It had grown darker and a little chilly. There was no more magic in the sky. It was as if someone had somewhere turned off the light on which all the illusion of the scene had depended. They walked back into the park. The band was playing an undulating tango. Mrs Knolles and the others were sitting on chairs under the trees. Anikin and Kathleen joined them and sat down. Neither of them spoke much during the rest of the evening. Presently Mrs Roseleigh joined them. She looked at Kathleen closely and there was a slight shade of wonder in her expression.

The next day Mrs Knolles had organized an expedition to the lakes. Kathleen, Anikin, Arkright, Princess Oulchikov and Count Tilsit were all of the party. When they reached the first lake, they separated into groups, Anikin and Kathleen, Count Tilsit and Mrs Roseleigh, while Arkright went with the Princess and Mrs Knolles.

Ever since the moment of magic at Bellevue, Kathleen had been like a person in a trance. She did not know whether she was happy or unhappy. She only felt she was being irresistibly impelled along a certain course. It is certain that her strange state of mind affected Anikin. It began to affect him from the moment he had held her in his arms on the hill and that the spell had so abruptly been broken. He had thought this had been due to the sudden interruption and the untimely intervention of the prosaic realities of life. But was this the explanation? Was it the arrival of the haberdasher on the scene that had broken the spell? Or was it something else? Something far more subtle and mysterious, something far more serious and deep?

Curiously enough Anikin had passed through, on that memorable evening, emotions closely akin to those which Kathleen had experienced. He said to himself: 'This is the Fairy Princess I have been seeking all my life.' But the morning after his moment of passion on the hill he began to wonder whether he had dreamed this.

And now that he was walking beside her along the broad road, under the trees of the dark forest, through which, every now and then, they caught a glimpse of the blue lake, he reflected that she was like what she had been *before* the decisive evening, only if anything still more aloof. He began to feel that she was eluding him and that he was pursuing a shadow. Just as he was thinking this ever so vaguely and tentatively, they came to a turn in the road. They were at a crossroads and they did not know which road to take. They paused a moment, and from a path on the side of the road the other members of the party emerged.

There was a brief consultation, and they were all mixed up once more. When they separated, Anikin found himself with Mrs Roseleigh. Mrs Knolles had sent Kathleen on with Count Tilsit.

Anikin was annoyed, but his manners were too good to allow him to show it. They walked on, and as soon as they began to talk Anikin forgot his annoyance. They talked of one thing and another and time rushed past them. This was the first time during Anikin's acquaintance with Mrs Roseleigh that he had ever had a real conversation with her. He all at once became aware that they had been talking for a long time and talking intimately. His conscience pricked him; but, so far from wanting to stop, he wanted to go on; and instead of their intimacy being accidental it became on his part intentional. That is to say, he allowed himself to listen to all that was not said, and he sent out himself silent wordless messages which he felt were received instantly on an invisible aerial.

For the moment he put all thoughts of what had happened away from him, and gave himself up to the enchantment of under-standing and being understood so easily, so lightly. He put up his feet and coasted down the long hill of a newly discovered intimacy.

Presently there was a further meeting and amalgamation of the group as they reached a famous view, and the party was reshuffled. This time Anikin was left to Kathleen. Was it actually disappointment he was feeling? Surely not; and yet he could not reach her. She was further off than ever and in their talk there were long silences, during which he began to reflect and to analyse with the fatal facility of his race for what is their national moral sport.

He reflected that except during those brief moments on the hill he had never seen Kathleen alive. He had known her well before, and their friendship had always had an element of easy sympathy about it, but she had never given him a glimpse of what was happening behind her beautiful mask, and no unspoken messages had passed between them. But just now during that last walk with Mrs Roseleigh, he recognized only too clearly that notes of a different and a far deeper intimacy had every now and then been struck accidentally and without his being aware of it at first, and then later consciously, and the response had been instantaneous and unerring.

And something began to whisper inside him: 'What if she is not the Fairy Princess after all, not your Fairy Princess?' And then there came another more insidious whisper which said: 'Your Fairy Princess would have been quite different, she would have been like Mrs Roseleigh, and now that can never be.'

The expedition, after some coffee at a wayside hotel, came to an end and they drove home in two motor cars.

Once more he was thrown together with Mrs Roseleigh, and once more the soul of each of them seemed to be fitted with an invisible aerial between which soundless messages, which needed neither visible channel nor hidden wire, passed uninterruptedly.

Anikin came back from that expedition a different man. All that night he did not sleep. He kept on repeating to himself: 'It was a mistake. I do not love her. I can never love her. It was an illusion: the spell and intoxication of a moment.' And then before his eyes the picture of Mrs Roseleigh stood out in startling detail, her melancholy, laughing, mocking eyes, her quick nervous laugh, her swift flashes of intuition. How she understood the shade of the shadow of what he meant!

And that mocking face seemed to say to him: 'You have made a mistake and you know it. You were spellbound for a moment by a face. It is a ravishing face, but the soul behind it is not your soul. You do not understand one another. You never will understand one another. There is an unpassable gulf between you. Do not make the mistake of sacrificing your happiness and hers as well to any silly and hollow phrases of honour. Do not follow the code of convention, follow the voice of your heart, your instincts that cannot go wrong. Tell her before it is too late. And she, she does not love you. She never will love you. She was spellbound, too, for the moment. But you have only to look at her now to see that the spell is broken and it will never come back, at least you will never bring it back. She is English, English to the core, although she looks like the illustration to some strange fairy tale, and you are a Slav. You cannot do without Russian comfort, the comfort of the mind, and she cannot do without English solidity. She will marry a squire or, perhaps, who knows, a man of business; but someone solid and rooted to the English soil and nested in the English conventions. What can you give her? Not even talent. Not even the disorder and excitement of a Bohemian life; only a restless voyage on the surface of life, and a thousand social and intellectual problems, only the capacity of understanding all that does not interest her.'

That is what the conjured-up face of Mrs Roseleigh seemed to say to him.

It was not, he said to himself, that he was in love or that he ever would be in love with Mrs Roseleigh. It was only that she had, by her quick sympathy, revealed his own feelings to himself. She had by her presence and her conversation given him the true perspective of things and let him see them in their true light, and in that perspective and in that light he saw clearly that he had made a mistake. He had mistaken a moment of intoxication for the authentic voice of passion. He had pursued a shadow. He had tried to bring to life a statue, and he had failed.

Then he thought that he was perhaps after all mistaken, that the next morning he would find that everything was as it had been before; but he did not sleep, and in the clear light of morning he realized quite clearly that he did not love Kathleen.

What was he to do? He was engaged to be married. Break it off? Tell her at once? It sounded so easy. It was in reality – it would be to him at any rate – so intensely difficult. He hated sharp situations.

He felt that his action had been irrevocable: that there was no way out of it. The chain around him was as thin as a spider's web. But would he have the necessary determination to make the effort of will to snap it? Nothing would be easier. She would probably understand. She would perhaps help him, and yet he felt he would never be able to make the slight gesture which would be enough to free him for ever from that delicate web of gossamer.

When Anikin got up after his restless and sleepless night he walked out into the park. The visitors were drinking the waters in the Pavilion and taking monotonous walks between each glass. Asham was sitting in a chair under the trees. His servant was reading out *The Times* to him. Anikin smiled rather bitterly to himself as he reflected how many little dramas, comedies and tragedies might be played in the immediate neighbourhood of that man without his being aware even of the smallest hint or suggestion of them. He sat down beside him. The servant left off reading and withdrew.

'Don't let me interrupt you,' said Anikin, but after a few moments he left Asham. He found he was unable to talk and went back to the hotel, where he drank his coffee and for a time he sat looking at the newspapers in the reading room of the Casino. Then he went back to the park. One thought possessed him, and one only. How was he to do it? Should he say it, or write? And what should he say or write? He caught sight of Arkright who was in the park by himself. He strolled up to him and they talked of yesterday's expedition. Arkright said there were some lakes further off than those they had visited, which were still more worth seeing. They were thinking of going there next week – perhaps Anikin would come too.

'I'm afraid not,' said Anikin. 'My plans are changed. I may have to go away.'

'To Russia?' asked Arkright.

'No, to Africa, perhaps,' said Anikin.

'It must be delightful,' said Arkright, 'to be like that, to be able to come and go when one wants to, just as one feels inclined, to start at a moment's notice for Rome or Moscow and to leave the day after one has arrived if one wishes to – to have no obligations, no ties, and to be at home everywhere all over Europe.'

Arkright thought of his rather bare flat in Artillery Mansions, the years of toil before a newspaper, let alone a publisher, would look at any of his manuscripts, and then the painful, slow journey up the stairs of recognition and the meagre substantial rewards that his so-called reputation, his 'place' in contemporary literature, had brought him; he thought of all the places he had not seen and which he would give worlds to see – Rome, Venice, Russia, the East, Spain, Seville; he thought of what all that would mean to him, of the unbounded wealth which was there waiting for him like ore in quarries in which he would never be allowed to dig; he reflected that he had worked for ten years before ever being able to go abroad at all, and that his furthest and fullest adventure had been a fortnight spent one Easter at a fireless *pension* in Florence. Whereas here was this rich and idle Russian who, if he pleased, could roam throughout Europe from one end to the other, who could take an apartment in Rome or a palace in Venice, for whom all the immense spaces of Russia were too small, and who could talk of suddenly going to Africa, as he, Arkright, could scarcely talk of going to Brighton.

'Life is very complicated sometimes,' said Anikin. 'Just when one thinks things are settled and simple and easy, and that one has turned over a new leaf of life, like a new clean sheet of blotting-paper, one suddenly sees it is not a clean sheet; blots from the old pages come oozing through – one can't get rid of the old sheets and the old blots. All one's life is written in indelible ink – that strong violet ink which nothing rubs out and which runs in the wet but never fades. The past is like a creditor who is always turning up with some old bill that one has forgotten. Perhaps the bill was paid, or one thought it was paid, but it wasn't paid – wasn't fully paid, and there the interest has gone on accumulating for years. And so, just as one thinks one is free, one finds oneself more caught than ever and obliged to cancel all one's new speculations because of the old debts, the old ties. That is what you call the wages of sin, I think. It isn't always necessarily what you would call a sin, but is the wages of the past and that is just as bad, just as strong at any rate. They have to be paid in full, those wages, one day or other, sooner or later.'

Arkright had not been an observer of human nature and a careful student of minute psychological shades and impressions for twenty years for nothing. He had had his eyes wide open during the last weeks, and Mrs Knolles had furnished him with the preliminary and fundamental data of her niece's case. He felt quite certain that something had taken place between Anikin and Kathleen. He felt the peculiar, the unmistakeable relation. And now that the Russian had served him up this neat discourse on the past he knew full well that he was not being told the truth. Anikin was suddenly going away. A week ago he had been perfectly happy and obviously in an intimate relation to Miss Farrel. Now he was suddenly leaving, possibly to Africa. What had happened? What was the cause of this sudden change of plan? He wanted to get out of whatever situation he found himself bound by. But he also wanted to find for others, at any rate, and possibly for himself as well, some excuse for getting out of it. And here the fundamental cunning and ingenious subtlety of his race was helping him. He was concocting a romance which might have been true, but which was, as a matter of fact, untrue. He was adding 'the little more'. He was inventing a former entanglement as an obstacle to his present engagements which he wanted to cancel.

Arkright knew that there had been a former entanglement in Anikin's life, but what Anikin did not know was that Arkright also knew that this entanglement was over.

'It is very awkward,' said Arkright, 'when the past and the present conflict.'

'Yes,' said Anikin, 'and very awkward when one is between two duties.'

'I think I have got him there,' thought Arkright. 'A French writer,' he said aloud, 'has said, *"de deux devoirs, il faut choisir le plus désagréable"*; that in choosing the disagreeable course you were likely to be right.'

Anikin remained pensive.

'What I find still more complicated,' he said, 'is when there is a right reason for doing a thing, but one can't use it because the right reason is not the real reason; there is another one as well.'

'For doing a duty,' said Arkright. 'Is that what you mean?'

'There are circumstances,' said Anikin, 'in which one could point to duty as a motive, but in which the duty happens to be the same as one's inclinations, and if one took a certain course it would not be because of the duty but because of the inclinations. So one can't any more talk or think of duty.'

'Then,' said Arkright, a little impatiently, 'we can cancel the word duty altogether. It is simply a case of choosing between duty and inclination.'

'No,' said Anikin, 'it is sometimes a case of choosing between a pleasure which is not contrary to duty (*et qui pourrait même avoir l'excuse du devoir*),' he lapsed into French, which was his habit when he found it difficult to express himself in English, 'and an obligation which is contrary both to duty and inclination.'

'What is the difference between an obligation and a duty?' asked Arkright. He wished to pin the elusive Slav down to something definite.

'Isn't there in life often a conflict between them?' asked Anikin. 'In practical life, I mean. You know Tennyson's lines:

"His honour rooted in dishonour stood
And faith unfaithful made him falsely
    true."

'Now I understand,' thought Arkright, 'he is going to pretend that he is in the position of Lancelot to Elaine, and plead a prior loyalty to a Guinevere that no longer counts.'

'I think,' he said, 'in that case one cannot help remaining "falsely true".' 'That is,' he thought, 'what he wants me to say.'

'One cannot, that is to say, disregard the

past,' said Anikin.

'No, one can't,' said Arkright, as if he had entirely accepted the Russian's complicated fiction.

He wanted, at the same time, to give him a hint that he was not quite so easily deceived as all that.

'Isn't it a curious thought,' he said, 'how often people invoke the engagements of a past which they have comfortably disregarded up to that moment when they no longer wish to face an obligation in the present, like a man who in order to avoid meeting a new debt suddenly points to an old debt as something sacred, which up till that moment he had completely disregarded, and indeed, forgotten?'

Anikin laughed.

'Why are you laughing?' asked Arkright.

'I am laughing at your intuition,' said Anikin. 'You novelists are terrible people.'

'He knows I have seen through him,' thought Arkright, 'and he doesn't mind. He wanted me to see through him the whole

181

time. He wants me to know that he knows I know, and he doesn't mind. I think that all this elaborate romance was perhaps only meant for me. He will choose some simpler means of breaking off his engagement with Miss Farrel than by pleading a past obligation. He is far subtler and deeper than I thought, subtler and deeper in his simplicity. I should not be surprised if he were to give her no explanation whatsoever.'

Arkright was in a sense right. What Anikin had said to Arkright was meant for him and not for Miss Farrel. It was not a rehearsal of a possible explanation for her, but it was the testing of a possible justification of himself to himself. He had not thought out what he was going to say before he began to talk to Arkright. He had begun with fact and had involuntarily embroidered the fact with fiction. It was *Wahrheit und Dichtung* and the *Dichtung* had got the better of the *Wahrheit*. His passion for make-belief and self-analysis had carried him away, and he had said things which might easily have been true and had hinted at difficulties which might have been his, but which, in reality, were purely imaginary. When he saw that Arkright had divined the truth, he laughed at the novelist's acuteness, and had let him see frankly that he realized he had been found out and that he did not mind.

It was cynical, if you called that cynicism. Anikin would not have called it something else: the absence of cement, which a Russian writer had said was the cardinal feature of the Russian character. He did not mean to say or do anything to Kathleen that could possibly seem slighting. He was far too gentle and far too easy-going, far too weak, if you will, to dream of doing anything of the kind. With her, infinite delicacy would be needed. He did not know whether he could break off his engagement at all, so great was his horror of ruptures, of cutting Gordian knots. This knot, in any case, could not be cut. It must be patiently unravelled if it was to be untied at all.

'I think,' said Arkright, 'that all these cases

are simple to reason about, but difficult to act on.' Anikin was once more amazed at the novelist's perception. He laughed again, the same puzzling, quizzical Slav laugh.

'You Russians,' said Arkright, 'find all these complicated questions of conflicting duties, divided conscience and clashing obligations, much easier than we do.'

'Why?' asked Anikin.

'Because you have a simple directness in dealing with subtle questions of this kind which is so complete and so transparent that it strikes us Westerners as being sometimes almost cynical.'

'Cynical?' said Anikin. 'I assure you I was not being cynical.'

He said this smiling so naturally and frankly that for a moment Arkright was puzzled. And Anikin had been quite honest in saying this. He could not have felt less cynical about the whole matter; at the same time he had not been able to help taking momentary enjoyment in Arkright's acute diagnosis of the case when it was put to him,

and at his swift deciphering of the hiero-
glyphics and his skilful diagnosis, and he had
not been able to help conveying the impression that he was taking a light-hearted view
of the matter, when, in reality, he was per-
plexed and distressed beyond measure; for
he still had no idea of what he was to do, and
the threads of gossamer seemed to bind him
more tightly than ever.

6

Anikin strolled away from Arkright, and as
he walked towards the Pavilion he met Mrs
Roseleigh. She saw at a glance that he had a
confidence to unload, and she determined
to take the situation in hand, to say what she
wanted to say to him before he would have
time to say anything to her. After he had
heard what she had to say he would no
longer want to make any more confidences,
and if he did, she would know how to deal
with them. They strolled along the *Galeries*

till they reached a shady seat where they sat down.

'You are out early,' he said, 'I particularly wanted–'

'I particularly wanted to see you this morning,' she said. 'I wanted to talk to you about Lancelot Stukely. You know his story?'

'Some of it,' said Anikin.

'He is going away.'

'Because of Donna Laura?'

'Oh, it's not that.'

'I thought he was devoted to her.'

'He likes her. He thinks she's a very good sort. So she is, but she's a lot of other things too.'

'He doesn't know that?'

'No, he doesn't know that.'

'You know how he wanted to marry Kathleen Farrel?' she said, after a moment's pause.

'Yes,' said Anikin, 'I heard a little about it.'

'It was impossible before.'

'Because of money?'

'Yes, but now it is possible. He's been left

money,' she explained. 'He's quite well off, he could marry at once.'

'But if he doesn't want to?'

'He does want to, that is just it.'

'Then why not? Because Miss Farrel does not like him?'

'Kathleen *does* like him *really;* at least she would like him really – only–'

'There has been a misunderstanding,' said Mrs Roseleigh. She put an anxious note into her voice, slightly lowering it, and pressing down as it were the soft pedal of sympathy and confidential intimacy.

'They have both misunderstood, you see; and one misunderstanding has reacted on the other. Perhaps you don't know the whole story?'

'Do tell it me,' he said. Once more he had the sensation of coasting or free-wheeling down a pleasant hill of perfect companionship.

'Many years ago,' said Mrs Roseleigh, 'she was engaged to Lancelot Stukely. She wouldn't marry him because she thought she couldn't leave her father. She couldn't have left him then. He depended on her for everything. But he died, and Lancelot, who was away, didn't come back and didn't write. He didn't dare, poor man! It was very silly of him. He thought he was too poor to offer her to share his poverty, but she wouldn't have minded. Anyhow he waited and time passed, and then the other day his uncle died and left him money, and he came back at once, and came here at once, to see her, not to see Donna Laura. That was just an accident, Donna Laura being here, but when he came here he thought Kathleen no longer cared, so he decided to go away without saying anything.

'Kathleen had been longing for him to come back, had been expecting him to come back for years. She had been waiting for years. She was not normal from excitement, and then she had a shock and disappointment. She was not, you see, herself. She was susceptible to all influences. She was magnetic for the moment, ready for an electric disturbance; she was like a watch that is taken near a dynamo on board ship, it makes it go wrong. And now she realizes that she is going wrong and that she won't go right till she is demagnetized.'

'Ah!' said Anikin, 'she realizes.'

'You see,' said Mrs Roseleigh gently, 'it wasn't anyone's fault. It just happened.'

'And how will she be demagnetized?' asked Anikin.

'Ah, that is just it,' said Mrs Roseleigh. 'We must all try and help her. We must all try to show her that we want to help. To show her that we understand.'

Anikin wondered whether Mrs Roseleigh was speaking on a full knowledge of the case, or whether she knew something and had guessed the rest.

'I suppose,' he said, 'you have always known what has happened to Miss Farrel?'

'I know everything that has happened to Kathleen,' she said. 'You see, I have known her for years. She's my best friend. And now I can judge just as well from what she doesn't say, as from what she says. She always tells me enough for it not to be necessary to tell me any more. If it was necessary, if I had any doubt, I could, and should always ask.'

'Then you think,' said Anikin, 'that she will marry Stukely?'

'In time, yes; but not at once.'

Anikin remembered Stukely's conduct and was puzzled.

'I am sure,' he said, 'that since he has been here he has made no effort.'

'Of course he didn't,' she said. 'He saw that it was useless. He knew at once.'

'Is he that kind of man, that knows at once?'

'Yes, he's that kind of man. He saw directly; directly he saw her, and he didn't say a word. He just settled to go.'

Anikin felt this was difficult to believe; all the more difficult because he wanted to believe it. Was Mrs Roseleigh making it easy, too easy?

'But he's going back to Africa,' he said.

'How do you know?' she asked.

'He told Mr Asham, and he told me.'

'He will go to London first. Kathleen will not stay here much longer either. I am going soon to London, too, and I shall see Lancelot Stukely there before he goes away, and do my best. And if you see him–'

'Before he goes?'

'Before he goes,' she went on, 'if you see him, perhaps you could help too, not by saying anything, of course, but sometimes one can help–'

'I have a dread,' said Anikin, 'of some explanations.'

'That is just what she doesn't want – explanations, neither he nor she,' said Mrs Roseleigh. 'Kathleen wants us to understand without explanations. She is praying we may understand without her having to explain to us, or without our having to explain to her. She wants to be spared all that. She has already been through such a lot. She is ashamed at appearing so contradictory. She knows I understand, but she doubts whether any one else ever could, and she does not know where to turn, nor what to do.'

'And when you go to London,' he asked, 'will you make it all right?'

'Oh yes,' she said.

'Are you quite sure you can make it all right? I mean with Stukely, of course,' he said.

'Of course,' said Mrs Roseleigh, but she knew perfectly well that he really meant all right with Kathleen.

'And you think he will marry her, and that she will marry him?' he asked one last time.

'I am quite sure of it,' she said, 'not at once, of course, but in time. We must give them time.'

'Very well,' he said. He did not feel quite sure that it was all right.

Mrs Roseleigh divined his uncertainty and his doubts.

'You see,' she said, 'what happened was very complicated. She knows that ever since Lancelot arrived, she was never really her-self–'

'She knows?' he asked.

'She only wants to get back to her normal self.'

'Well,' he said, 'I believe you know best. I will do what you tell me. I was thinking of going to London myself,' he added. 'Do you think that would be a good plan? I might see Stukely. I might even travel with him.'

'That,' said Mrs Roseleigh, 'would be an excellent plan.'

Mrs Roseleigh's explanation, the explanation she had just served out to Anikin, was, as far as she was concerned, a curious blend of fact and fiction; of honesty and disingenuousness. She was convinced that both Kathleen and Anikin had made a mistake, and that the sooner the mistake was rectified the better for both of them. She thought if it was rectified, there was every chance of Stukely marrying Kathleen, but she had no reason to suppose that her explanation of his conduct was the true one. She thought Stukely had forgotten all about Kathleen, but there was no reason that he should not be brought back into the old groove. A little management would do it. He would have to marry now. He would want to marry; and it would be the natural, normal thing for him to marry Kathleen, if he could be persuaded that she had never cared for anyone else; and Mrs Roseleigh felt quite ready to undertake the explanation. She was quite disinterested with regard to Kathleen and quite disinterested towards Stukely. Was she quite disinterested towards Anikin?

She would not have admitted to her dearest friend, not even to herself, that she was not; but as a matter of fact she had consciously or unconsciously annexed Anikin. He was made to be charmed by her. She was not in the least in love with him, and she did not think he was in love with her; she was not a dynamo deranging a watch; she was a magnet attracting a piece of steel; but she had not done it on purpose. She had done it because she couldn't help it. Her conscience was quite clear, because she was convinced she was helping Kathleen, Stukely and Anikin out of a difficult and an impossible situation; but at the same time (and this is what she would not have admitted) she was pleasing herself.

Their conversation was interrupted by the arrival first of Kathleen herself, then of Arkright.

Kathleen had in her hands the copy of a weekly review.

After mutual salutations had passed, Kathleen and Arkright sat down near Mrs Roseleigh and Anikin.

'Aunt Elsie,' said Kathleen to Arkright, 'asked me to give you back this. She is not coming down yet, she is very busy.' She handed Arkright the review.

'Ah!' said Arkright. 'Did the article on Nietzsche interest her?'

'Very much, I think,' said Kathleen, 'but I liked the story best. The story about the brass ring.'

'A sentimental story, wasn't it?' said Arkright.

'What was it about?' asked Anikin.

'Mr Arkright will tell it you better than I can,' said Kathleen.

'I am afraid I don't remember it well enough,' said Arkright.

He remembered the story sufficiently well, although being of no literary importance, it had small interest for him; but he saw that Miss Farrel had some reason for wanting it told, and for telling it herself, so he pressed her to indicate the subject.

'Well,' she said, 'it's about a man who had been all sorts of things: a soldier, a king, and a savant, and who wants to go into a monastery, and says he had done with all that the world can give, and as he says this to the abbot, a brass ring, which he wears round his neck, falls on to the floor of the cell. The ring had been given him by a queen whom he had loved, a long time ago, at a distance and without telling her or anyone, and who had been dead for years. The abbot tells him to throw it away and he can't. He gives up the idea of entering the monastery and goes away to wander

196

through the world. I think he was right not to throw away the ring, don't you?' she said.

'Do you think one ought never to throw away the brass ring?' said Anikin, with the incomparable Slav facility for 'catching on', who instantly adopted the phrase as a symbol of the past.

'Never,' said Kathleen.

'Whatever it entails?' Anikin asked.

'Whatever it entails,' she answered.

'Have you never thrown away your brass ring?' asked Anikin, smiling.

'I haven't got one to throw away,' she said.

'Then I will send you one from London. I am going there in a day or two,' he said.

'Mrs Roseleigh was right,' he said to himself, 'no explanations are necessary.'

Mrs Roseleigh looked at him with approval. Kathleen Farrel seemed relieved too, as though a weight too heavy for her to bear had been lifted from her, as though after having forced herself to keep awake in an alien world and an unfamiliar sunlight, she was now allowed to go back once more to the region of dreamless limbo.

'Yes,' she said, 'please send me one from London,' as if there were nothing surprising or unexpected about his departure.

In truth she was relieved. The episode at Bellevue was as far away from her now as the dreams and adventure of her childhood. She felt no regret. She asked for no explanation. Anikin's words gave her no pang; nothing but a joyless relief; but it was with the slightest tinge of melancholy that she realized that she must be different from other people, and she would not have had things otherwise.

As Arkright looked at her dark hair, her haunting eyes and her listless face, he thought of the Sleeping Beauty in the wood; and wondered whether a Fairy Prince would one day awaken her to life. He did not know her full story; he did not know that she was a mortal who had trespassed in Fairyland and was now paying the penalty.

The enchanted thickets were closing round her, and the forest was taking its revenge on the intruder who had once rashly dared to violate its secrecy.

He did not know that Kathleen Farrel had in more senses than one been overlooked.

PART TWO

THE PAPERS OF ANTHONY KAY
(cont.)

CHAPTER II

Dr Sabran read the papers I sent him the very same night he received them, and the following evening he asked me to dinner, and after dinner we sat on the verandah of his terrace and discussed the story.

'I recognized Haréville,' said Dr Sabran, 'of course, although his Saint-Yves-les-Bains might just as well have been any other watering-place in the world. I do not know his heroine, nor her aunt, even by sight, because I only arrived at Haréville two years ago after they had left, and last year I was absent. Princess Kouragine I have met in Paris. She and yourself therefore are the only two characters in the book whom I know.'

'He bored Princess Kouragine,' I said.

'Yes,' said Sabran, 'that is why he has to invent a Slav microbe to explain her indifference. But Mrs Lennox flattered him?'

'Very thoroughly,' I said.

'Well, the first thing I want to know is,' said Sabran, 'what happened? What happened then? but first of all, what happened afterwards?'

I said I knew little. All I knew was that Miss Brandon was still unmarried; that Canning went back to Africa, stayed out his time, and had then come back to England last year; and that I had heard from Kranitski once or twice from Africa, but for the last ten months I had heard nothing, either from or of him.

'But,' I said, 'before I say anything, I want you to tell me what you think happened and why it happened.'

'Well,' said the doctor, 'to begin with, I understand, both from your story as well as from his, that Kranitski and Miss Brandon were engaged to be married and that the engagement was broken off. But I also understood from your MS that the man Canning was for nothing in the rupture of the engagement. It happened before he arrived. It was due, in my opinion, to something which happened to Kranitski.

'Now, what do we know about Kranitski as related by you? First of all, that he was for a long time attached to a Russian lady who was married, and who would not divorce because of her children.

'Then, from what he told you, we know that although a believing Catholic he said he had been outside the Church for seven years. That meant, obviously, that he had not been *pratiquant*. That is exactly what would have happened if he had been living with a married woman and meant to go on doing so. Then when he arrives at Haréville, he tells you that the obstacle to his practising his religion no longer exists. Kranitski makes the acquaintance of Miss Brandon, or rather renews his old acquaintance with her, and becomes intimate with her. Princess Kouragine finds she is becoming a different being. You go away for a month, and when you come back she almost tells you she is engaged – it is the same as if she told you. The very next day Kranitski meets you, about to spend a day at the lakes with Miss Brandon and evidently not sad – on the contrary. He received a letter in your presence. You are aware after he has read this letter of a sudden change in him.

'Then a few days later he comes to see you and announces a change of plans, and says he is going to Africa. He also gives you to understand that the obstacle has not come back into his life. What obstacle? It can only be one thing, the obstacle he told you of, which was preventing him from practising his religion.

'Now, what do we learn from the novel?

'We learn from the novel that the day after that expedition to the lakes, Rudd describes the Russian having a conversation with the novelist (himself) in which he tells the novelist, firstly, that he is going away, probably to Africa. So far we know that he was telling the truth. Then he says that just as he found himself, as he thought, free, an old debt or tie or obligation rises up from the past which has to be paid or regarded or met. Rudd, in the person of Arkright, thinks he is inventing. They talk of conflicts and divided duties and the choice between two duties. The Russian is made to say that the most difficult complication is when duty and pleasure are both on one side and an obligation is on the other side, and one has to choose between them. The novelist gives no explanation of this, he treats it merely as a gratuitous piece of embroidery – a fantasy.

'Now, I believe the Russian said what Rudd makes him say, because if he didn't it doesn't seem to me like the kind of fantasy the novelist would have invented had he been inventing. If he had been inventing, I think he would have found something else.'

'All the same,' I interrupted, 'we don't know whether he said that.'

'We don't know whether he said anything at all,' said Sabran.

'I know they had a conversation,' I said,

'because I was in the park all that morning and someone told me they were talking to each other. On the other hand, he may have invented the whole thing, as Rudd says that the novelist in his story knew about the Russian's former entanglement, and lays stress on the fact that the Russian did not know that he knew. So it may have been on that little basis of fact that all this fancywork was built.'

'I think,' said Sabran, 'that the conversation did take place. And I think that it happened so. I think he spoke about the past and said that thing about the blotting-paper. There is a poem of Pushkin's about the impossibility of wiping out the past.'

'And I think,' I said, 'that the Russian laughed, and said, "You novelists are terrible people." Only he was laughing at the novelist's density and not applauding his intuition.'

'Well, then,' said Sabran, 'let us postulate that the Russian did say what he was reported to have said to the novelist, and let us conclude that what he said was true.'

'In that case, the Russian said he was in the position of choosing between a pleasure, that is to say, something he wanted to do which was not contrary to his duty–'

'For which duty might even be pleaded as an excuse,' said Sabran, quoting the very words said to have been used by the Russian.

'And an obligation which was contrary both to duty and to inclination. That is to say, there is something he wants to do. He could say it was his duty to do it. And there is something he doesn't want to do, and he can say it is contrary to his duty. And yet he feels he has got to do it. It is an obligation, something which binds him.'

'It is the old liaison,' said Sabran.

'In that case,' I said, 'why did he go to Africa?'

'Yes, why did he go to Africa? And stay there at any rate such a long time. Did he talk of coming back?'

'No, he said nothing about coming back.

He said he liked the country and the life, but he said little about either. He wrote chiefly about books and abstract ideas.'

'Perhaps,' said Sabran, 'there is something else in his life which we know nothing about. There is another reason why I do not think that the old liaison is the obligation. He took the trouble to come and see you before he went away and to tell you that the obstacle which had prevented his practising his religion had not reappeared in his life. It is probable that he was speaking the truth. And he knew he was going to Africa. So it must be something else.'

'Perhaps,' I said, 'it was something to do with Canning. What are your theories about Canning, the other man?'

'What are yours?' he said. 'I heard nothing about him.'

I said I thought that all Mrs Summer had told me about Canning was true. Rudd, I explained to Sabran, disliked Mrs Summer, and had drawn a portrait of her as a swooping gentle harpy, which I knew to be quite false. 'Although,' I said, 'I think the things he makes her say about Canning are quite true. I think he reports her thoughts correctly but attributes to her the wrong motives for saying them. I don't believe she ever talked to him about Canning; but he knew her ideas on the subject, through Mrs Lennox. I believe that Canning arrived at Haréville on purpose to see Miss Brandon. I know that the Italian lady had played no part in his life and that it was just a chance that they met at Haréville. I believe he arrived full of hope, and that when he saw Miss Brandon he realized the situation as soon as he had spoken to her. This is what Rudd makes Mrs Summer say, and I believe that is what happened. In Rudd's version of Mrs Summer she is lying. Rudd had already a preconceived notion that Miss Brandon's first love was to forget her. He had made up his mind about that long before the young man came upon the scene, before he knew he was coming on the scene, and when he did, he distorted the facts to suit his fiction.'

'Then,' said Sabran, 'his ideas about Miss Brandon. All that idea of her being the "Princess without dreams", without passion, being muffled and half-awake – "overlooked", as he says, which I suppose means *ensorcelée.*'

I told him I thought that was not only fiction but perfectly baseless fiction. I reminded him of what Princess Kouragine had said about Miss Brandon.

'I must think it over,' said Sabran. 'For the present I do not see any completely satisfactory solution. I am convinced of one thing only, and that is that the novelist drew false deductions from facts which were perhaps sometimes correctly observed.'

I said I agreed with him. Rudd's deductions were wrong; his facts were probably right in some cases; Sabran's deductions were right, I thought, as far as they went; but we either had not enough facts or not enough intuition to arrive at a solution of the problem.

As I was saying this, Sabran interrupted me and said:

'If we only knew what was in the letter that the Russian received when he was with you we should have the key of the enigma. It was from the moment that he received that letter that he was different, wasn't it?'

I said this was so, and what happened afterwards proved that it was not my imagination.

'What in the world can have been in that letter?' said Sabran.

I said I did not think we should ever know that.

'Probably not,' he said, musingly. 'And that incident about the story of the Brass Ring. Do you think that happened? Did they say all that?'

I was able to tell him exactly what had happened with regard to that incident.

'I was sitting in the garden. It was, I think, the morning after they had all been to the lakes, and about the middle of the day, after the band had stopped playing, shortly before *déjeuner*, that Rudd, Miss Brandon, Kranitski and Mrs Summer all came and talked to me before I went into the hotel.

'Miss Brandon gave the copy of the *Saturday Review*, or whatever the newspaper was, back to Rudd, and mentioned the story of the Brass Ring, and they discussed it, and I asked what it was about. Rudd was asked to read it aloud to us, and he did. Miss Brandon and Kranitski made no comments; and Rudd asked Kranitski if he thought the man had done right to throw away his ring, and Kranitski said: "A chain is no stronger than its weakest link."

'Rudd said: "Perhaps the brass ring was the strongest link."

'Kranitski and Miss Brandon said nothing, and Mrs Summer said she was glad the man had not thrown the ring away. Then Rudd asked Miss Brandon whether she had ever thrown away her brass ring.

'Miss Brandon said she hadn't got one, and changed the subject. Then they all left me. That was all that happened.'

'I understand,' said Sabran; 'that is interesting, and it helps us to understand the methods of the novelist. But we are still no nearer a solution. I must think it over. *Que diable y avait-il dans cette lettre?'*

CHAPTER III

The more I thought over the whole story the more puzzling it seemed to me. The puzzle was increased rather than simplified by a letter which I received from Kranitski from Africa, in which he expressed no intention of coming back, but said he was living by himself, quite contented in his solitude.

I told Sabran of this letter and the Doctor said we were without one important *donnée*, some probably quite simple fact which would be the clue of the whole situation: the contents of the letter Kranitski had received when he was with me–

'What we want,' he said, 'is a moral Sherlock Holmes, to deduce what was in that letter–'

It was after I had been at Haréville about ten days, that Sabran asked me whether I would like to make the acquaintance of a Countess Yaskov. She was staying at Haréville and was taking the waters. He had only lately made her acquaintance himself, but she was dining with him and he wanted to ask a few people to meet her. I asked him what she was like. He said she was not exactly pretty, but gentle and attractive. He said: *'Elle n'est pas vraiment jolie, mais elle a une jolie taille, de beaux yeux, et des perles.'*

She had been divorced from her husband for years and lived generally at Rome, so he had been told.

I went to Sabran's dinner. There were several people there. I had never met Countess Yaskov before. She seemed to be a very pleasant and agreeable lady. I sat next to her. She was an accomplished musician, and she played the pianoforte after dinner with a ravishing touch. She was certainly gentle, intelligent, and natural. We were talking of Italy, when she astonished me by saying she had not been there for some time. Later on she astonished me still more by talking of her husband in the most natural way in the world. But I had heard cases of Russians being divorced and yet continuing to be good friends. I longed to ask her if she knew Kranitski, but I could not bring his name across my lips. I asked her if she knew Princess Kouragine. She said, 'Which one?' And when I explained or tried to describe the one I knew, there turned out to be about a dozen Princess Kouragines scattered all over Europe; some of them Russian and some of them not, so we did not get any further, and Countess Yaskov was vagueness itself.

We talked of every conceivable subject. As she was going away she asked Sabran if he could lend her a book. He lent her Rudd's *Unfinished Dramas*, and asked me if he might lend her *Overlooked*. I said certainly, but I explained that it was more or less a private book about real people.

Two or three days later I met her in the park. She asked me if I had read Rudd's story. I told her it had been read to me.

'But it is meant to happen here, isn't it?' she said. 'And aren't you one of the characters?'

I said this was, I believed, the case.

'Then you were here when all that happened?' she said. 'Did it happen like that, or was it all an invention?'

I said I thought there was some basis of fact in the story, and a great deal of fancy, but I really didn't know. I did not wish to let her know at once how much I knew.

'Novelists,' I said, 'invent a great deal on a very slender basis, especially James Rudd.'

'You know him?' she said. 'He was here with you, of course?'

I told her I had made his acquaintance here, but that I had never seen him before or since.

'What sort of man is he?' she asked.

I gave her a colourless, but favourable portrait of Rudd.

'And the young lady?' she said, 'Miss – I've forgotten her name.'

'The heroine?' I asked.

'Yes, the heroine who is "overlooked". Do you think she was "overlooked"?'

'In what sense?'

'In the fairy-tale sense.'

I said I thought that was all fancy-work.

'I wonder,' she said, 'if she married the young man.'

'Which one?'

'The Englishman.'

I said I had not heard of her being married.

'And was there a Russian here, too?' she asked.

'Yes,' I said, 'his name was Kranitski.'

'That sounds like a Polish name.'

I said he was a Russian.

'You knew him, too?'

'Just a little.'

'It is an interesting story,' she said, 'but I think Rudd makes all the characters more complicated than they probably were. Does Mr Rudd know Russia?'

I said I believed not at all.

'I thought not,' she said.

I said that Kranitski seemed to me a far simpler character than Rudd's Anikin.

'Did Dr Sabran know all those people?' she asked.

I said Dr Sabran had not been here while it was going on.

'It would be very annoying for that poor girl to find herself in a book,' she said, 'if he published it.'

I said that Rudd would probably never publish it – although he would probably deny that he had made portraits, and to some extent with reason, as his Kathleen Farrel was quite unlike Miss Brandon.

'Oh, her name was Miss Brandon,' Countess Yaskov said, pensively. 'If she comes here this year you must introduce me to her. I think I should like her.'

'Everyone said she was beautiful,' I said.

'One sees that from the novel. I suppose James Rudd invented a character which he thought suited her face.'

I said that that was exactly what had happened. Rudd had started with a theory about Miss Brandon, that she was such and such person, and he distorted the facts till they fitted with his theory. At least, that was what I imagined to have been the case.

I asked Countess Yaskov what she thought of the psychology of Rudd's Russian. I said she ought to be a good judge. She laughed and said:

'Yes, I ought to be a good judge. I think he is rather severe on the Slavs, don't you? He makes that poor Anikin so very complicated, and so very sly and fickle as well.'

I said I thought the excuses which Rudd credited the Russian with making to himself for breaking off the engagement with the heroine of the book, were absurd.

'Do you think the Russian said those things or that the novelist invented them?' she asked.

I said I thought he had said what he was reported to have said.

'If he said that, he was not lying,' she said.

I agreed, and I also thought he *had* said all that; but that Rudd's explanation of his words was wrong. If that was true he must have broken off his engagement.

'There is nothing very improbable in that, is there?' she asked.

'Nothing,' I said. And yet I thought that Kranitski had finished with whatever there was in the past that might have been an obstacle to his present.

'Did he tell you that?' she asked.

As she said that, although the tone of her voice was quite natural, almost too natural, there was a peculiar intonation in the way she said the word 'he', in that word and that word only, which gave me the curious sensation of a veil being lifted. I felt I was looking through a hole in the clouds. I felt certain that Countess Yaskov had known Kranitski.

'He never told me one word that had anything to do with what Rudd tells in his novel,' I said.

I felt that my voice was no longer natural as I said this. There was a strain in it. There was a pause. I do not know why I now felt certain that Countess Yaskov possessed the key of the mystery. I suddenly felt she was the woman whom Kranitski had known and loved for seven years, so much so, that I could say nothing further. I also felt that she knew that I knew. We talked of other things. In the course of the conversation I asked her if she thought of staying a long time at Haréville.

'It depends on my husband,' she said. 'I don't know yet whether he is coming here to fetch me, or whether he wants me to meet him. At any rate I shall go back to Russia for my boys' holidays. I have two sons at school.'

The next time I saw Sabran I asked him what he had meant by telling me that Countess Yaskov was divorced from her husband. I told him what she had said to me about her husband and her sons. He did not seem greatly surprised; but he stuck to his point that she was divorced.

The next time I saw Countess Yaskov, she told me she had told a friend of hers about Rudd's story. Her friend had instantly recognized the character of Anikin.

'My friend tells me,' she said, 'that the novelist is quite false as far as that character is concerned, false and not fair. She said what happened was this: the man whom Rudd describes as Anikin had been in love for many years with a married woman. She was in love with him, too, but she did not want to divorce her husband, for various reasons. So they separated. They separated after having known each other a long time. Then the woman changed her mind and she settled she would divorce, and she let Anikin know. She wrote to him and said she was willing, at last, to divorce. My friend says it was complicated by other things as well. She did not tell me the whole story, but the man went to Africa and the woman did not divorce. What Anikin was supposed to have said to the novelist was true. He told the truth, and the novelist thought he was saying false things. That is what you thought, too. But all has been for the best in the end, because do you know what there is in today's *Daily Mail?*' she asked.

I said no one had read me the newsp
as yet.

'The marriage is announced,' she said, 'o
Miss Brandon to a man called Sir Somebody Canning.'

'That,' said I, 'is the Englishman in the
book.'

'So Mr Rudd was wrong altogether,' she
said, and she laughed.

That is all that passed between us on this
occasion, and I think this is a literal and
complete transcription of our conversation.
Countess Yaskov told me her story, the
narrative of her friend, with perfect naturalness and with a quiet ease. She talked as if
she were relating *facts* that had no particular
personal interest for her. There was not a
tremor in her voice, not an intonation, either
of satisfaction or pain, nothing but the quiet
impersonal interest one feels for people in a
book. She might have been discussing Anna
Karenina, or a character of Stendhal. She
was neutral and impartial, an interested but
completely disinterested spectator.

of her voice was subtly different
had been the other day towards
ır conversation. For during that
ͻ admirably natural as she had
ͻeen, and although her voice only betrayed
her in the intonation of one syllable, I feel
now, looking back on it, that she was not
sure of herself, that she knew she was walking the whole time on the edge of a
precipice.

This time I felt she was quite sure of herself; sure of her part. She was word-perfect
and serenely confident.

Of course, what she said startled me. First
of all, the *soidisant* explanation of her friend.
Had she told a friend about the story? I
thought not. Indeed, I feel now quite certain
that the friend was an invention, quite certain that she knew I had recognized her as
the missing factor in the drama, and that
she had wished me not to have a false impression of Kranitski. But at the time, while
she was talking she seemed so natural that
for the moment I believed, or almost

believed, in the friend. But when she told me of Miss Brandon's marriage she furnished me with the explanation of her perfect acting, if it was acting. I thought it was the possession of this piece of news which enabled her to tell me that story so calmly and so dispassionately.

Of course I may still be quite wrong. I may be seeing too much. Perhaps she had nothing to do with Kranitski, and perhaps she did tell a friend. She has friends here.

Nevertheless I felt certain during our first conversation, at the moment I felt I was looking through the clouds, that she had been aware of it; aware that I had not been able to go on talking of the story as naturally as I had done before. Her explanation, what her friend was supposed to have said, fitted in exactly with my suppositions, and with what I already knew. Sabran had been right. The clue to the whole thing was the letter. The letter that Kranitski had received when he was talking to me and which had made so sudden a change in him was the letter from her, from Countess Yaskov, saying she was ready to divorce and to marry him. He received this letter just after he was engaged to be married to Miss Brandon. It put him in a terrible situation. This situation fitted exactly with what Rudd made him say to the novelist in the story: his obligation to the past conflicted with his inclination, namely, his desire to marry Miss Brandon.

Of course I might be quite wrong. It might all be my imagination. The next day I got a belated letter, from Miss Brandon, for-warded from Cadenabbia, telling me of her engagement. She said they were to be married at once, quite quietly. She knew it was no use asking me, but if I had been in London, etc. She made no other comments.

That evening I dined with Sabran. I told him the news about Miss Brandon, and I told him what Countess Yaskov had told me her friend had told her about the story.

'Half the problem is solved,' he said. 'The story of Countess Yaskov's friend explains the words which Rudd lends to the Russian.

His inclination, which was to marry Miss Brandon, coincides with the religious duty of a *croyant*, which is not to marry a divorcée, and not to put himself once more outside the pale of the Church, but it clashes with his obligation, which is to be faithful to his friend of seven years. His inclination coincides with his duty, but his duty is in conflict with his obligation. What does he do? He goes away. Does he explain? Who knows? He was, indeed, in a *fichu* situation. And now Miss Brandon marries the young man. Either she had loved him all the time, or else, feeling her romance was over, she was marrying to be married. In any case, her novel, so far from being ended, is only just beginning. And the Russian? Was it a real amour or a *coup-de-tête*? Time will show. For himself he thought it was only a *coup-de-tête*: he will go back to his first love, but she will never divorce.'

I asked him again whether he was sure that Countess Yaskov was divorced from her husband. He was quite positive. He knew it *de source certaine.* She had been divorced years ago, and she lived at Rome. I was puzzled. In that case, why did she try and deceive me, and at the same time if she wanted to deceive me why did she tell me so much? Why did she give me the key of the problem? I said nothing of that to Sabran. I saw it was no use.

A few days later, Countess Yaskov left Haréville. She told me she was going to join her husband. I did not remain long at Haréville after that. A few days before I left, Princess Kouragine arrived. I told her about Miss Brandon's marriage. She said she was not surprised. Canning deserved to marry her for having waited so long. 'But,' she said, 'he will never light that lamp.'

I asked her if she was sorry for Kranitski. She said:

'*Very*, but it could not be otherwise.'

That is all she said. When I told her that I had made the acquaintance of Countess Yaskov, she said:

'Which one?'

I said it was the one who lived in Rome and who was separated from her husband.

The next day she said to me: 'You were mistaken about Countess Yaskov. The Countess Yaskov who was here is Countess *Irina* Yaskov. She is not divorced, and she lives in Russia now. The one you mean is Countess Hélène Yaskov. She lives at Rome. They are not relations even. You confused the two, because they both at different times lived at Rome.' I now saw why I had been put off the scent for a moment by Sabran. I asked her if she knew my Countess Yaskov. She said she had met her, but did not know her well.

'She is a quiet woman,' she said. *'On dit qu'elle est charmante.'*

Just about this time I received a long letter from Rudd. He said he must publish *Overlooked*. He had been told he ought to publish it by everybody. He might, he said, just as well publish it, since printing five hundred copies and circulating them privately was in reality courting the maximum of publicity:

the maximum in quality if not in quantity. By doing this, one made sure that the only people it might matter reading the book, read it. He did not care who saw it, in the provinces, in Australia, or in America The people who mattered, and the only people who mattered, were friends, acquaintances and the London literary world, and now they had all seen it. Besides which, his series of unfinished dramas would be incomplete without it; and he did not think it was *fair* on his publisher to leave out *Overlooked*. 'Besides which,' he said, 'it is not as if the characters in the books were portraits. You know better than anyone that this is not so.' He ended up, after making it excruciatingly clear that he had irrevocably and finally made up his mind to publish, by asking my advice; that is to say, he wanted me to say that I agreed with him. I wrote to him and said that I quite understood why he had settled to publish the story, and I referred to Miss Brandon's marriage at the end of my letter.

Before I heard from him again, I was called away from Haréville, and I had to leave in a hurry. It was lucky I did so, because I got away only just in time, either to avoid being compelled to remain at Haréville for a far longer time than I should have wished to do, or from having to take part in a desperate struggle for escape. The date of my departure was July 27th, 1914.

The morning I left I said goodbye to Princess Kouragine, and I reminded her that when I had said goodbye to her two years ago she had said to me, talking of Miss Brandon: 'The man behaved well.' I asked her which man she had meant. She said:

'I meant the other one.'

'Which do you call the other one?' I asked.

She said she meant by the other one:

'*Le grand amoureux.*'

I said I didn't know which of the two was the '*grand amoureux.*'

'Oh, if you don't know that you know nothing,' she said.

At that moment I had to go. The motor

bus was starting.

I feel that Princess Kouragine was right and that, after all, perhaps I know nothing.

The publishers hope that this book has given you enjoyable reading. Large Print Books are especially designed to be as easy to see and hold as possible. If you wish a complete list of our books please ask at your local library or write directly to:

Dales Large Print Books
Magna House, Long Preston,
Skipton, North Yorkshire.
BD23 4ND